MW01641112

ONE D R O P: TO BE THE COLOR BLACK

By
Xennia Gittoes-Singh
a.k.a. ~~~Running Waters~~~

Revised
2nd Printing

One Drop:
To Be the Color Black

PART 1:
One Black Skinned Woman's Poems on Racism in the 20th Century

A Collection
By
Xennia Gittoes-Singh

Second Edition
Second Printing

ISBN 0-7414-1662-X

Lil' Mike Press
PO Box 206
Hartfield, VA 23071
Xenpoet2@aol.com

Previously Published Works include
Mother Earth's Daughter

Published by:

519 West Lancaster Avenue
Haverford, PA 19041-1413
Info@buybooksontheweb.com
www.buybooksontheweb.com
Toll-free (877) BUY BOOK
Local Phone (610) 520-2500
Fax (610) 519-0261

Printed in the United States of America

Printed on Recycled Paper

Published August 2003

DEDICATED TO

my ancestors
who have borne the brunt of their `race'... either by being born too black or too white to fit in with any `race'.

my peers
who embraced their race and heritage and took to the streets for the right to learn and celebrate their `racial' identities and histories.

my heirs
who will inherit our definitions of our human race.

One Drop: To Be the Color Black

Part I:

One Black Skinned Woman's
Poems on Racism
in the 20th Century

CONTENTS

Part I

One Drop: To Be the Color Black

Part II:

My White Skinned Friends' Poems on Racism for the 21st Century

Part II

PEOPLE / INFLUENCES

FEELINGS / POV / MY PERSPECTIVE

PERSONAL / TESTIMONIES

Xennia works very hard to create harmony in a world we are told is full of dysfunction. This woman, this poet, this friend has not led the easiest of lives, yet her approach to life is one of love without cliché. And her concept for this anthology, that of exchanging viewpoints on race from some of her rather paler friends is nothing short of brilliant and furthers her cause.

In this precious volume, that you hold in your hands lies the secrets of the universe, poets doing what they do best writing poems to create a better world, or shock people out of indifference, and then smiling upon one another.

Larry Jaffe
Author, Poet, Co-founder Poets for Peace,
"Unprotected Poetry," "Jewish Soulfood," "Hates not Natural," "Eating the Rain"

The reader of One Drop: To Be the Color Black *has no choice other than to examine his or her feelings and values regarding race while they absorb the knowledge and wisdom within these pages. After being bombarded by* Little Tommy Jefferson *(who is credited with crafting the 'one drop' rules) and the first hand account of American racism in public places in* Daddy Mack, *Xennia makes us confront the truth and remember,* Lest We Forget, *our historical legacy. Xennia's multi-cultural, multi-ethnic approach to the subject of race is refreshing, as she encourages us all to clarify our values and* Live the Dream.

Sharon Smith- Knight
Author, Poet, Teacher
"The Man Who Doesn't Live Here Anymore," "Wine Sip" and "Animal Magnetism 1&2"

One Drop: To Be the Color Black *is a much-needed collection of poems that forces us to take a hard look at racism in America. In Part 1, we see the powerful voice of Gittoes-Singh examining her own life as a woman of mixed blood whose daily interactions with others have largely been defined by skin color. In Part 11, she presents a collection of poems by her "white skinned friends" whose views on racism point to the poignant paradox of Einstein-there is no such thing as race because it is virtually impossible to trace back far enough to determine every drop of blood that comprises our being. Ultimately, Gittoes– Singh hopes that racism will one day be eradicated and replaced by a harmonious world in which we all live together as one race, as humankind.*

Carolyn Kreiter-Foronda, Ph.D.
Poet, Artist and Educator
Virginia Cultural Laureate, 1992
"Contrary Visions," "Death Comes Rising"

"Blessed are the peacemakers..." In an act of peace and healing, Xennia Gittoes-Singh brings many voices into harmony on the subject of racism. The significance of this collection extends beyond its important topic. Xennia has invented a model for literary dialogue in which her prose commentary moderates and unifies an innovative range of Spoken Word poetry. Not only has she made a ground-breaking contribution to U.S. literature; she has created a genre.

Denise De Vries
Author, "The Disappearance of Bobo Blando," "Hispanic Culture Review," co-editor

"We are told, too, that white blood is superior,
but in the same breathe informed
that one 'drop' of 'Negro' blood
makes a white man a Negro,
which is equivalent to saying
that if a citizen has ninety-nine white ancestors and one black,
that one drop
cancels
all
that the whites have contributed."

J. A. Rogers in his book entitled Sex and Race, Volume III, page 277

(The editor placed the emphasis on words and changed the paragraph structure. The words are Mr. Rodgers'…xl)

Acknowledgments

To my heroes J. A. Rogers for Sex & Race Volumes I, II, & III, Ivan Van Sertima, Cheikh Anta Diop, Camus, Muhammad `Ata ur-Rahim, Lerone Bennent, Zachariah Sitchen, Graham Hancock, Donald Johanson, Michael Edey and other scholars and authors to numerous to name who whet my thirst for knowledge.

During my lifetime I have met a lot of people who were well known for their accomplishments. When I have met such people I have thought, this is something I will tell my grandchildren. Many people say it is not what you know, but who you know. I say that it is not who you know, but how they know you. I have seen in person or have actually met and talked with some ...some of them know me ...and some I have forgotten. I acknowledge them and what they have achieved during their lives. Thanks to all of you for being around in my lifetime.

ONE DROP: TO BE THE COLOR BLACK
Part 1
One Black Skinned Woman's
Poems on Racism
in the 20th Century

Dear Grandchildren,
i have gathered together a collection of poetry that i have been writing since i was about 9 years old...
i wanted to share this collection of poetry with you...
i have moved a lot over the years and i have lost many journals of my work...
i wrote One Drop, the poem in the 60's...thank goodness it's an easy piece to remember...
i have forgotten so many...
and that's why i am putting these poems in book form for you now...
i want to get them written down and off my aging hard drive (brain)...
grand momma needs more ram ☺...

i have been blessed, my babies...
grand momma has been blessed...
to be able to read, research, write and express my thoughts freely...
NEVER take that for granted...
it wasn't always true for me...
i, just like many generations of people before me, have gotten into trouble for expressing my inner thoughts verbally...
i believe there is no such thing as race for human beings...
i believe we are all one race, the human race...
it may sound corny, or simplistic...
however, most real Truths are...

very simple…
i believe you must take a stand for what you believe…
live each day as though it is your last…

thus, this collection of poetry is meant to cause dialogue among you…
it is meant to stimulate discussion and research…
to teach you, grandchildren to grant your fellow man …
respect and understanding…
while i don't believe there is 'no such thing as race…
there are many people and places that do…

racism is an institution, its 'ism' seeped into almost every fiber of our international consciousness...
racism is a system of oppression for a social purpose…
the original purpose of racism was to justify slavery and its enormous economic benefits…
unlike being biased which means showing favoritism, inclination, preference
or being prejudiced which means to have premature judgment, partiality or to injure or harm by action…
these are the definitions I am using for this collection…

the most important thing about keeping our freedom of speech, to me…
is learning how to listen …
racism is painful and hurts all parties involved…
on a one to one level, we know that when we hurt someone's feelings, ignoring them doesn't help to solve the problem…
saying, forget about it, doesn't make it go away...

ultimately, communication is a major key to solving the problem and helps to alleviate some of the pain…

these poems represent impressions that i made on the world as i see it and the impressions that the world made on me, so far…
i offer no explanations or excuses for these words…

i will approximate the dates that i wrote after each poem…
i pretend to represent and speak for no one but myself…
this collection of my poems, my grandchildren is `race' as i experienced it in the 20th Century...
my life… my experiences… right or wrong….

LOVE & kisses,

Grand Xennia
~~~Running Waters~~~

My grandchildren are Stephanie Shakara Cole, Nicholas Brown and Blair Alexander Tucker. Also my god-grands Elijah Heath, and Zion Ray Whitt…this one is for U and the future grandchildren i can't wait to meet. If i get to heaven before you, i'll save you a spot.

Intro:

Way back when

I believe I was about five or six years old when I discovered two life changing things about myself. #1. I had black skin. #2. I was considered a "NIGGER."

It was a very confusing time for me. I soon learned that the girl that broke the news to me by calling me that N word, was black, too. Never mind that she didn't look black. Her skin was white. She was a 'red-bone' or 'hi yella' as my aunt explained. None of it made sense to me. My skin was clearly not black. I was bronze or tan or mocha or cocoa or something I couldn't describe and the girl was pink, yet no one was called pink or brown. It was really confusing.

Upon reflection, it was unusual for a girl like me not to know her skin color by the age of two, as I was in the fifties. Unfortunately, I have been reminded numerous times of my skin-tone as an American. The confusion deepened when I was reunited with my Dad after being separated from him when I was about 4 or 5 years old. He re-entered my life when I was 19 years old.

Daddy was upset when he observed my book collection and realized I was very interested in African - American history. I can still feel my hand in his as he told me that he had kidnapped me when I was younger so that I wouldn't be raised as a "nigger." Believe me I was shocked! What did my father think I was? What did my father think he was? Why he was a nigger too! Surely he knew that.

He didn't know that. He was raised in Panama and Jamaica. He was a merchant seaman and traveled all over the world. He was accepted for being a man first. Then he was accepted for being an Indian man from Japore, India, and Colon, Panama, and Kingston, Jamaica. He was a Singh and everyone knew he was a Caucasian, an Aryan, a Sikh. So what if his skin color was darker than mine. He spoke with an accent, his hair was straight and he carried a passport. So there.

So there lay the very reason my mom said she left me and Dad years ago in New York City. I recalled her words about her and Dad's reasons for not living together. She said he didn't understand her American blackness. The black experience for a black native born American woman was dramatically different from a man's of any race..

My mother was very sensitive to her race and her sex as she was constantly reminded to keep her place as a citizen of the 1930's to 50's. She explained how Dad would try to teach her to speak with an accent, to wrap and wear a sari, to wear a bindi on her forehead so she could escape the prohibitive racism still running rampant in our America. He wanted her to be able to sit anywhere on the train going to a funeral for her relative from New York to North Carolina. No Jim Crow car for his woman.

Of course, she didn't want to wear the sari or the bindi or speak with an accent. She endured the pain of her blackness and it ripped them apart. No, it wasn't the only thing that caused them to break up but it was enough for my mother to use as a reason for why I never saw my father when I was a young girl of 4 and older, but that's another book.

This book, this collection has evolved from the cooling pot of my ancestors lineage and the cauldron of the time and place in which I was born. My friend Linda Lopez, (I love you Linda even though we don't talk often) reminded me a few years ago of a racist incidence we encountered years ago which may summarize my true feelings about living in a society that believes in racial categories. Linda and I had lost contact for a few years. I called to wish her a happy holiday or because I had found her number or for some reason out of the blue.

Linda says, "Girlfriend, I was just telling some of my friends about you and about that racist incident we had a while back."

"What racist incident?" I asked, trying to recall.

"You remember" she replied, "the one you, Bill, Larry and I experienced when we went up to my sister's cabin in Big Bear?"

"No, remind me." I said, not remembering.

"How could you not remember!" she said incredulously. "That incident changed my life. I never will forget it ...how could you forget, just get over it, that's amazing!"

To make a long story short, the man called me the `N' word for no reason. Linda defended me vigorously. I forgot about it, and that's the point. I don't necessarily remember everything a sexist said or did to me either. There are mean, rude people in every culture and color of skin has nothing to do with it. There are a lot of people that pretend they are better than everyone else for one reason or other. Often, race is just a handy way to start trouble. A hot button to push, a buzz word to use.

Luckily the human genetic code has been broken. There is scientific proof of Einstein's theory, now in the year 2000. All men share 99.9% similar DNA regardless of their skin color. There is no such thing as race.

AFRICA, THE MOTHER

Africa, the Mother of this earth,
Man's oldest bones were found there first
and all the world's knowledge can be trased back there
we tend to forget, but let's make this clear
the black woman is the mother of us all
so sista's teach us to stand tall and proud
to raise your fist and proclaim out loud
I bow down to her royalness

Isis, Nefertiti, Cleopatra and such
all lived lives that we imitate much
yet our kids remain ignorant to the truth
they argue and complain because we give them no roots
I'm RoyalTee the Princess of Rhyme*
my main goal is to honor mankind
you see, without the black woman there would be no way
that I could stand before you and shout and say
take some time to think today
there's really got to be a better way

the future of our blackness is a cause of derision
we need black leaders making life changing decisions
we need to remember Africa, our mother
remember to honor her and love her
give her the respect that is due all Queen Mothers'
then, bow down to her royalness.

**RoyalTee- My daughter, Nicole Lynette Tuckers' stage name. This is a rap song I wrote for her in 1989. Princess of Rhyme was the name of her rap album released in 1988.*

A COLORED, NEGRO, AFRICAN-AMERICAN, BLACK SPIRITUAL

Were you there when they sacrificed my race? Were you there? Did you watch them refuse me service at Denny's? Did you stand by when they said I couldn't attend your school? Did you stay home when they voted no to affirmative action? Were you there?

Were you there when they interred my people in concentration camps, when a bomb was dropped on Pearl Harbor? Were you there when the United States continued to do business with apartheid South Africa? Were you there?

Were you there when they injected black men with syphilis in Tuskegee? Were you there when they refused to feed healthy black newborn babies in the 1990's in Baltimore? Were you there?

Were you there when they paid women 40% less for the same career? When they red-lined your neighborhood? Were you there?

Were you there when they had no books for my classroom? Were you there when we shared a computer with the whole school while white children had a computer for every student? Were you there when the white tenured teachers stopped teaching me? Were you there?

Were you there when they said Rodney King was attacking the policeman that had him on the ground handcuffed? Were you there to see people `upraising' all *over the world on TV until they cut the feedtube satellite and gave us a 'race riot' in LA? Were you there?*

Oh sometimes, sometimes it makes me want to shake you, wake you? Were you there when they sacrificed my race? Were you there?

(written 1960's revised for this collection)

FREESHADE

Stare out my window
stare at Freeshade
stare at auction block
see slaves, black babies, for sale
black men, black women at a discount
people for sale at Freeshade
Freeshade has humans for sale

Stare at the Rappahannock
Stare at the smooth water
Stare at the boats coming in
See the Indians watching from shore
wise men's prophesies fulfilled
waishus coming

The People killed at
Mills Creek Landing
to make room for
horses and cows
Mills Creek Landing left
with houses standing
The People gone
who knows where

Stare at the woods
Stare at the fields
Stare down the roads
See the Red and Black People
running . . .
running from the man
who is white with greed

Staring at the ghosts
of the people from
*Freeshade and Mills Creek Landing**
staring out
my window.....

**Freeshade and Mills Creek Landing are located in Hartfield, Middlesex County, Virginia. Hartfield is approximately 30 miles north of Jamestown where black slaves were first brought into the United States. Staring out my bedroom window I can see the stump of a hanging tree and the garage in the Robinsons' yard which used to be an auction block for the sale of slaves.*
(written 1980's)

DADDY MACK

It was a hot country day and I had decided that today, this very day, I would go to the movies.

I was 12 years old and I had never been to the movies. That was ridiculous! Today, all that would change. My campaign to see a movie began.

I approached Daddy Mack as soon as his old pick-up truck pulled into the yard.
"I want to go to the movies, Daddy" I pleaded.
"We went to the drive-in last week," Daddy said "I never go to the movies here."
"What?" I said, "The drive-in is not the same. A movie is different. I want to go."
I begged. I pleaded for what seemed to me like hours.

You see, this would be a huge treat for me. I had never been to a movie and until last week I had never been to a drive-in. Daddy Mack and Mommie Eva had no way to know what my home life had been like in my northern small town. They didn't know that I had never watched television or seen a movie because of my aunt and grandmother's religious beliefs.

Now that I was in Virginia and my caretakers were far away in New Jersey, I had no fear they would discover I had broken this cardinal rule they had imposed. I was free. They would never find out what I was doing way down here in the south. I could see a movie at long last!

Finally and reluctantly, Daddy Mack agreed to take me to the movies. Mommie Eva refused to go which I found odd as she liked to get out, as she would say, "To take a ride in the evenings."

We got into the car for the long ride into town. Daddy Mack shared the story of how he and Mommie Eva brought me to Virginia when I was three years old. He related how he and Mommie had won me in a card game. He said that he and Mommie planned to keep me in the country. Then he would go into the now familiar story of how he and mom lost me. The day my real mother decided on a whim to come down south and claim me as her child. How she grabbed me out of Mommie Eva's arms and ran to a waiting car and drove away with me. How I screamed for Mommie Eva how I cried and screamed banging my little hands and arms on the rear window. How Mommie has nightmares of my cries.

I heard his voice crack as he recounted the way he came home much later and found me gone and Mommie numb with pain and grief. How he grabbed his shotgun and climbed into this very truck and rode up and down the roads looking for me day and night for weeks, tears streaming down his face, as he rode, looking for the car that took me away from him.

Daddy Mack reminded me that he and Mommie searched for me every year in that northern city until they found me playing hopscotch outside my grandmother's house. The same house they had gotten me from years earlier. He said it was a miracle that they found me at last this summer and he and Mommie never wanted to lose me again. That he said was the only reason he agreed to take me to the movies in town.

At last, we pulled up to the theater. I was so . . . excited! It was so cool, man. As soon as we stepped inside I was welcomed by cool air conditioning, which was unheard of in those days. The lobby was plush with royal red carpets on the floor and walls decorated with ornate ornaments. There was a huge counter with every candy imaginable and the lobby had a heavenly smell that Daddy Mack defined as popcorn.

But . . . we couldn't have any popcorn. We couldn't have any candy or drinks. He said in a very small strange sounding voice. A stained voice that caused me to look at him for the first time that evening, I mean really look at him. He turned and headed for a small dark staircase in the rear of the lobby.
"Come along." he said.
I followed, my eyes glancing about and settling on the sign above the stairs.

The sign. I saw the sign. I read the sign. My mind reeled. Tears sprang to my eyes as the words sank in. "Colored Only" the sign read. I read the words out loud. COLORED ONLY. The words echoed, reverberated in that cavernous room. Colored only,only,only...colored...

Daddy Mack seemed to shrink from his six foot two stature. His shoulders slooped, his feet dragged as though the bottoms were lined with glue. He climbed the stairs slowly. I pulled myself up after him. We reached the landing. Daddy looked at me.
"I have never been in here. Please..." he said, "never ask me to do this again."
My heart sank to the pit of my stomach. I thought I would retch. I wanted to retch. I wanted to disappear, to turn

around and run, to leave this horrible place. How could I put this wonderful man through this pain, this humiliation for a lousy, stupid movie.

Somehow, we got home. I remember spending the evening lying prostrate on my bedroom floor. Praying the way my aunt and my grandmother taught me when you have truly sinned. . Praying that God would forgive me for insulting the only man that truly loved me, my Daddy Mack.

My first theater. My first movie. My first time out alone with my new found Dad. I can remember as plain as day the pain on his face, the pain in his voice. I can only remember how I made a good man, a loving man. Take humiliation and pain for something trivial that I wanted to do.

And somehow, no matter how hard I try to think . . . I just can't seem to remember, no, I just can't seem to recall the name of that movie.

THE OTHER RACE

Race is not a skin color
race is a state of mind
race is a culture
race is a notion made up by greedy men
men seeking power, evil men
race is not a skin color

It's easy to prove this theory for yourself
just have a family reunion
and invite all the family ...
(yes, even the `other' family members)
or, fill out a application for anything
and there will always be the question . . .
What is your race? Choose one.

Then there will be three boxes
white always first
black
then
other

What does other mean?
What color is an other?
What race is an other?
Is it a color we haven't decided on yet?
Who will decide what race an other will be?

Perhaps we should consider race
as a culture, not a color.
Maybe it would be better
to ask people what culture
they would embrace

on an application.
What would be the purpose
of such a question?
What is the purpose of asking about race?
My blood brother was born with white skin
he checks the white box
my nephew has black skin and a white mother
he checks the white box
my grandson has white skin he has a white father
he checks the black box

What race is Justice Clarence Thomas?
His beautiful skin color, on television
is three shades blacker
than a brand new black Lexus
but his ideology is white
Clarence Thomas should check the white box.

Ward Connerly and Larry Elder
should check the white box
A lot of black skin men and women
should check the white box
Eminem should check the black box
many white skin men and women should
check the black box, you see
Race is not a skin color
Race is a state of mind

It is so confusing
White/Black/Other
there are so many others
indeed almost everyone I know is an other
which is an undefined race
and an undisclosed color

Maybe we can decide the next race of man
these others should be.
I say every other should look,
well . . .
they should all look
just like me. ☺

(written 1990's)

WHO AM I ON ST. PADDY'S DAY?

Because my grandfather was a red headed man with a full beard who answered to the name Thomas O'Daugherty, I reserve the right to lean head over heels to kiss the Blarney Stone and wear the green, on this day that honors St. Paddy.

Perhaps he too was as black as was rumored. Yes. As black as the black Irish, as black and green as me or thee, oh gee "top `o the morn' to ya." Just can't forget my Irish genes.

So let me remove my fathers' fathers' bindi from my forehead, before I become mistaken for the pure Aryan Sikh that I am. Lest black Krishna and white Indra fought for nothing and there is no such thing as race. Ah yes, Irish I'll be today.

Wearing the green, a perfect colleen, a lass who loves all things Irish. It means today I won't be Cherokee. Not me. Not today. Don't bring me a form today and ask me my race. I don't want to see that dumb look on your face when I check the white box Irish.

Today, I'm not French 's'il vous plait', nor African American, by the way. No today, today I'm Irish. So you take the low road and I'll take the high road and I'll get to the Truth before ya'. I'll stay on the red road, I'll stay Waken Taken, I'll ease on down the Irish road today. Cause today, oh today, I am Irish.
(written 1990's)

I MARCHED FOR YOU

There are songs that can mark definite moments in your life. This song reminds me of the good `ole days when I belonged to the NAACP.

"I believe the children are the future. Teach them well and let them lead the way. Show them all the beauty they possess inside, give them a sense of pride to make it easier…"

I marched for you. I marched for you,
I stood there defiantly and I sang
I would hold the hands of other people

Young and old, black and white
We would cross our arms, hold hands and sing
"We shall overcome, We shall overcome. . ."

Many times we sang with tears streaming down our faces
I was young, I believed I could make a difference
I marched for you, I sat in, I stood up for what I believed

I defied my parents
Defied my elders
I took to the streets, to march for freedom

As we marched we would sing
To make the walk easier
To make the distances seem shorter we sang

When they released the dogs, we sang, I sang
"I shall not, I shall not be moved. I shall not, I shall not be moved. Just like a tree planted by the water, I shall not be moved."

I marched for our children,
I marched for our parents and our ancestors,
I marched for you, grandchildren

When they sprayed us with hoses and locked up our friends, we sang, I sang
"Paul and Silas bound in jail, had no money to pay the bail, keep your eyes on the prize, hold on, hold on . . ."

I marched for you, children. I marched so that things would be different. I knew I could make a difference. Instead . . . the people like us . . .
the foot soldiers

have disappeared
behind rocks, drugs, prison walls,
behind corporations, politics, progress

I marched for you.
I sat in. I stood up.
I sang for the grandchildren and for you

"Let the children's laughter remind us how it used to be..."

I marched for you and today grandchildren, my grandchildren, our grandchildren, are still being called nigger, still dragged into restrooms raped and killed, still dragged behind trucks until their limbs fall off

our children... still discriminated against and hated for the color of their skin. "There is no more affirmative action," you say, "There are no more privileges for being born black. Oh no, not today. Only privileges and life as usual for white men."

I marched for you. I sat in. I stood up. I sang.
"Oh freedom, Oh freedom, Oh freedom over me and before I'll be a slave, i'll be buried in my grave and go home to my Lord and be free."

I marched for you, I sat in. I stood up. I put my life on the line. I risked being labeled by the FBI. Risked being black balled by the white owned corporations

I marched for you, I went to college for you, I voted for you. I worked in corporations for you.
To make this world a better place. And, for what?

I marched for you, went to jail for you,
I sat in, I stood up.
I went to war for you because I loved you.

I put my life on the line. I was ready to die. Kill me
Not for Nikes or the latest name brand shoes, or the color of my clothing. Not for a neighborhood that doesn't belong to me

I marched so you could work, could vote
I sang so you could go to school, learn, teach
I stood up for what I believed in

I marched, I sat in
I sang
I stood up for you...now please babies, take the torch.

VIETNAM'S FORGOTTEN VICTIMS

The minority woman left behind, watching their men die on TV, during the evening meal. War at six p.m. Watch your brother, your cousin, your father, your uncle, your nephew if he is a minority living in America . . . watch him die on the killing fields of Vietnam. He'll die for your enjoyment, for your pleasure. He'll die to keep you safe and warm in your segregated gated enclaves at home in America. Just after this commercial, we'll return to War in Vietnam.

For your immediate pleasure, we'll have black and brown Johnny marching off to war. Whole classes of graduating black men, the cream of the crop., marching. Cream or not just be healthy you can be a drop out, it doesn't matter after eight weeks boot camp, we will have you ready to kill another brown man for black gold. Have you ready to protect the oil rights in the oil fields belonging to one Rockefellow family.

'Cause I remember you, Kent Jordon at your goodbye party. You had just graduated from high school. I can still see you grinding you girlfriend against the wall. "For your love oh I would do anything, oh I would go anywhere, for your love." I can hear your momma yelling down the stairs to us..." turn those lights back up and turn that music down."

I can still taste the kool-aid and the potato chips (no dip in those days). You walked me home after the party. You told me that I was pretty. You said you would visit me after the boot camp. You kissed me so gently. I

remember, your lips on my neck, on my ear, brushing my cheek, buzzing my lips. Sweet butter-fly kisses.
But I was away when you came home briefly and you left for Vietnam. Returning a year later in a flag draped box. Given a huge funeral for the distinction of being the first in our small town to die for the conflict . . .the skirmish, the little misunderstanding abroad. Why it wasn't a war, you know, not declared, not so anyone knew . . .

I watched you George, painting my bedroom that Halloween orange, reflecting on your clean-cut looks. Your broad shoulders, your slim waist, your high tight buns and those strong thighs . . . painting, painting, painting . . . Your preacher father having plenty of reason to be proud of you. Innocence exudes from you. Optimism is your friend. Your face has quick smiles and your eyes light up a room. Your infectious energy gets you paid handsomely for your volunteer paint job.

You bound off for boot camp where you spend eight intense weeks. You fly off to the Mekong Delta. You write long informative letters . . . the Quonset huts, the insects, the Vietnamese cleaning woman raped by your fellow fighters, the weather, the rain, the rain, the stinking rain. Then, shorter letters, soon, no letters.

A year and a half later I see someone who looks somewhat like you around the corner from where I live. Sitting on a bus stop, a brother in army fatigues. An older version of George. A man with a scraggly beard and vacant eyes. Our eyes meet, a moment of recognition,
"It's you, George, why didn't you say you were home? George, is it you?"

"Hi sweet Lady," you say," just home for a minute. Been to rehab, baby. I fell into Vietnam drug fields, baby. They got the best shit there, baby. Oh yeah, I got hooked, I got hurt, I got humped back home. Didn't want you to see me like this, the family doesn't know I'm home. Cause I'm home and I'm hooked. No place to go but back to the Nam, do you understand? They have the best shit the purest heroin and we need it. It makes us fearless. We do anything, kill any one. They have the best shit . . . did I tell you? I'm going back."

George died in Vietnam. He came home wrapped in a body bag, in a flag draped coffin.

We went to so many funerals the minority women, at least, two to six a month, funerals for our men. The invisible victims of an undeclared war.
The brown and the black soldiers mothers, sisters, girlfriends, cousins, friends, wives the forgotten victims of the not- a- war in Vietnam.

And sometimes I wonder. Are their names on the wall? Have you seen it? That Vietnam Memorial Wall. Tell me, is Kent Jordan's name on the Wall, is George's name on the Wall? Are my fifteen to twenty personal loved ones names on the Wall? You see I can't stand to look at that Wall I am always blinded by my tears. I'm too afraid I'll see their names. Will you look for me? If you see them will you touch them, caress them, kiss their names for me the forgotten victims of the not- a- war in Vietnam. Are their names on the Wall?

Vietnam's Legacy

The Vietnam War raged on and on…not all the minority men died fighting the War. Some left babies behind in Vietnam. Black unwanted children abandoned, ignored and left to fend for themselves.

No, not all the men died in Vietnam. Some came home blind, crippled or crazed. They were made blind by their war dreams, crippled by the war reality and crazed by the scorn heaped on them from the Americans they supposedly fought to keep free.

The minority woman left behind fought one another for the few decent men left behind or the men sent home.

They raised the children the men could never father.

Woman left with little to choose from for fathers, leaders, role-models or hero's in their race.

Woman forced to work for 2/3rds less pay than anyone else earned in America, including non-citizens.

Women forced to accept television for daycare as they worked for below minimum wage jobs while their children were advertised into wanting things their mothers could never afford to buy.

Women impoverished and asked to go manless for food and health care for their children from Big Daddy Welfare.

Woman left to raise children ripe for government supplied heroin, cocaine and various other street drugs.
Women blamed for the gap between them and their men as they fought each other for the same affirmative action positions or careers.

Women left to raise the children destined to live or work in the concentration camps / jails / prisons the government continues to build for the children of the men who may have been their fathers, their hero's.

Women who watched the men who were the cream of the crop, the men on the top, the brightest and the healthiest die on TV during the evening meal.

Yet the minority women refused to be victims.
They bore the cross of their burdens and they persevered.
They worked many jobs and raised good children.
New progeny for a new millenium, children still filled with hope and love for their country and their countrymen.
The woman who had no time to cry, to lie down and die or to ask anyone who, what or why?
The minority women who loved
the minority men who fought
the not- a- war
in Vietnam
(1980 revised 1990's)

ONE DROP: TO BE THE COLOR BLACK

Black
a color
black
all colors
black
every color in the spectrum
to be the color black

One drop, one drop, one drop black

one drop black on black makes all black
one drop red on black makes all black
one drop yellow on black makes all black
one drop white on black makes all black

one drop, one drop, one drop black

white
no color
white
devoid of all color
white
the absence of color
to be the color white

one drop, one drop, one drop black

one drop white on white makes all white
one drop red on white makes all red
one drop yellow on white makes all yellow
one drop black on white makes all black

one drop, one drop, one drop black

white woman
has eggs of one color
white man
makes babies of one color

Black woman
has eggs of every color
black man
makes babies of every color

one drop, one drop, one drop black

Black
a color
black
all colors
black
every color in the spectrum
to be the color black

Now don't argue with me
thank your great white father
Thomas Jefferson for the rules

To be
or not to be
are you
BLACK?

(1963)

POW WOW

We can see them from the top of the hill as we are arriving
we hear the drum beats and we can feel the dancers jumps
through the bottoms of our feet
listen to the drumbeats
listen to the songs of the tribe, of the clan

the colors of the rainbow flash in front of our eyes
plumes, feathers of every color
representing many birds, flowers, animals
orange, green, purple, red, bright yellow, pink,
flying through the air

Dancers dressed like peacocks
men walk around preening their feathers
bells jingling, jangling as
they prance by us
dressed in full regalia

Watch them dance and become
the buffalo, the eagle, the bison, the enemy
see the women dance with
purple, yellow, red, green blankets representing
clan and family.

Many people lined up for
brown fry bread with white powdered sugar
red tomatoes, green lettuce on Navajo taco's
brown and black buffalo burgers,
yellow and white corn
Displays and vendors

hawking bleached white
animal bones
brown -white tanned
animal skins

Red, orange swathed women
bells ringing around shapely hips
wrists, thighs, ankles
hair adorning feathers, barrettes,
combs of yellow, lime- green, brown, black, turquoise

Feet clad in pretty moccasins
beaded white, sky blue, red
embroidered purple, yellow
to dance intertribal dances
clan dances on red earth

Colors blaze,
colors adorn, colors blink
colors command the day of the Pow Wow
colors represented in all
but the Indians

Indians colors changed
from black, brown, red to white
now, mostly white Indians
in charge, living large
at the Pow
Wow!!!

(1990's)

JUBA

June 19, 1998

JUBA!!! JUBA!!! JUBA!!!*
I'S FREE!! I'S FREE!!!
It's one hundred and thirty three,
one hundred and thirty three years to this day
June 19, 1865 now known as Juneteenth

So what it if it took eighteen months to two years
to notify slaves like me
what difference does it make
when you was tole
ifn now yous free?

Yeah, it's 1998
133 years to this date
and I a black living in America
still suffer from
aparthate

See I's free, I's free
to be pulled over for DWB
in your community
I's free to be harassed
for driving, shopping, walking while black
in America

I am free to be beaten
by a hundred police,
I am free to be pulled from
behind a truck
until my limbs fall off

free to have our trader
uncle toms paid top dollar
to ridicule blacks daily
on radio, television. Spanked daily on the Internet
and in print media by manipulated black coons

free to live with
American taught
Aparthate
133 years to the date
when the slaves was freed.

Juba, juba, whoopee, whee
We's free in1998

**JUBA a celebration, party, jubilee*

(1998)

MY FRIED CHICKEN POEM

I sat down to write
this funny poem
This poem that would entertain you
Be light and bright ; not blame you

Poems that tell you I could lick you up,
Eat you with a spoon
Suck you like a bone
Love you night and day
until the cows come home

Instead I choose this poem to say
Africa is just 15 miles away
15 miles away from Europe
yet historians would like us to think
and say Africa is a million miles away

you tell me not to say these things out loud
just go along with the crowd
fiddle and laugh while Rome burns
sit and watch them drop bombs
in Philadelphia & Waco homes

spend my time before you
talking about my fantasy lovers
how I dream of buff
good looking
revolutionary brothers

political prisoners
are a fact of life
don't talk about them in
a poem
it just ain't right

What does it matter where Africa is
America is where we live
Lets talk about concerns of today
Let what happened in the past stay
That way

Who cares if King James did
Every thing that he could to
Make Europeans feel
proud and good,
it's true

As they were making slaves out of the very
People whose history they read in the Bible
Greedy kings and popes knew
that if they hid the truth real good
No one would ever dare to make them libel

No this is my fried chicken poem
The poem that tells you
I can go uptown, downtown
All around the town
With my sexual partner

To tell you I been around the world in 80
hou...80 minit...
oh, OK 80 seconds
He's was a one second brother
But that's another poem

This is my grease drippin', finger lickin'
Big buttermilk biscuit dippin' poem
The one that's bound to make you holler and scream
While I spend my 15 minutes of fame
Helping you to defile black woman's name

Telling you my but is a hut, what I like to suck
As though I didn't know if someone
Dropped a dime this very minute
Cops would be all over us, walking up these steps in riot gear
Makin' us confess that, yeah, we done it, we done it, whatever, dear

Yeah, this is my fried chicken poem
My let me entertain you poem
Tell me are you enjoying me, are you panting ?
am I getting you wet?
Tell me,
are we having FUN yet?

SEX AND RACE

Sex and race,
sex and race
doncha know it
populate the place

De president Clinton
he say
people talk race,
people say

mon, shut yo' face
we would rather
speak of sex instead
let's talk about gettin' head

sex and race,
sex and race
doncha know it
populate the place

ain't it funny
how media get's it high
it uses sex
as stimuli

it needs to hype
it's sales
needs lots of gore
and sexy tales

race ain't my problem, they say
now sex we can twik
it a subject that's fun
we can talk tongue n cheek

we can talk tongue and come
knee pads and all
but race ain't a subject
I want to recall

if you wish to talk race again
I will show you a rope my friend
and we can hang ya high
see if race can fly in the sky

sex and race,
sex and race
doncha know it
populate the place

You see as long as sex is here
race is such a bore even tho'
sex and race sex and race
populate the place

race and violence
might be all right
we could discuss that
subject all night

But discuss race
oh how ho hum
it wasn't my fault
it's over, it's done

who cares if
sex and race
sex and race
populate this crazy place

Sex an' Lewinsky
now that's nice and juicy
Clinton in South Africa
I'd rather talk budget in Biafra

there really is
no such thing as race
to think there is
is a real disgrace

So many races having
sex, sex, sex
it really makes
race purists vexed

because sex and race,
sex and race
really helps to
populate the place

(1999)

MOTHER NATION

MY HERO

WINNIE MANDELA

I first saw her standing like a flower among a sea, an ocean of children. A beautiful, youthful looking woman surrounded by waves of dancing, singing children. Children raising their fists and dancing their dance, abandla...hu, hu, hu, abandla, hu, hu, hu. It was awesome. Could it be that such a young woman was married for 20 or more years to a man who had been in prison for most of them? I still remember...

I saw you standing there fist in the air, Winnie
standing by your man, your country
being strong, trying to right the things
you knew were wrong

You are a mighty warrior,
Mother Mandela
a beautiful example
for our daughters

Winnie, some powerful white men
have tried the same old games
they always use on women of color
when we speak our minds with conviction

They always say we are wrong
angry, ranting, raving, bitchy when we women play
men's games with men's rules
and win, some men complain.

How well we know
all is fair in love and war

you loved your husband, your children
and your nation enough to make the ultimate sacrifice.

You stood by and for a man and a country
for a long time in your life
you sacrificed your youth and your happiness
for others pain and strife
You are the general
who won the war in South Africa
yet they accuse you of standing around
while an alleged traitor martyred his life for his country

Many a great warrior
many a great general would be proud
if they had only shed the blood of one individual
for the good of, the future of, a whole nation

You and the children
took a stand
and you bravely
changed the world

You and South Africa's beautiful children
won a long hard fought war
with nothing but sticks, stones, matches
hopes, dreams and the Truth.

The children call you
Mother Nation
Mother Nation
I adore you
Abandla, abanndla, abandla

(1990's)

Lest We Forget

Remember
the sales of human beings,
stinking slave ships
blacks killing themselves & their loved one's
to be free

remember
stealing Native American lands
looting and plundering their natural resources
forcing Native American's to live
on reservations

remember
forcing Hebrews to wear the Star of David
poison gas showers at Bitburg
making lampshades from
human flesh

remember
inoculating unknowing men with syphilis
allowing black babies to stave in Boston hospitals
twenty policemen needed
to beat one man

remember
white man killing white men
because they are
the wrong
Kind of
white

remember
black men selling
black men

because that was
always right
remember
the homeless man
you walked by
the abused child who's eyes make you
want to cry

remember
the first bomb dropped
on American soil
in the city of
brotherly love
where even the liberty bell broke when tolled...

remember
Mandella
aparthate
political prisoners
Mumia Abul Jumar

remember Leonard Peltier
greasy grass,
Dee Brown telling you and me about
Burying our hearts
at Wounded Knee

Each day we are living
we are dying if
we are denying
we need to remember
lest we forget

(1960's revised for this collection)

ONE MAN, ONE VOTE BLUES

Ron Reagun was elected President
before I got to vote
yes, this was in California
no, all of us ain't dopes

I should have gotten to the polls earlier
however, my job got in the way
I just can't seem to pay my bills
if I don't work for pay

there is no way that I wouldn't go
I couldn't be a no show
too many people fought and died
for me to stay at home and hide

so I pulled into my polling place
the church lights brightened up my face
when I heard the announcement on my radio
"Ron Reagun is President," "Oh no," I say

This can't be true, how can this be?
How could America decide this without me
The polls weren't closed in California yet
Could we put our ballots in the boxes
Before you start cashing in your bets?

Is this a democracy?
What happened to one man, one vote?
Are we speaking the same language here?
Did I just get off a boat?

And this electoral college thing
No one truly understands
Does it let you tell folks before the polls are closed
That Ron Reagun is their man

So I went into the polling site
As mad as hell
Announcing loudly so that all could hear
Something in our government smells

Pinch me I say aren't you people here
Preparing to vote, just like me
Why is Ron Reagun grinning and announcing
He is President on TV?

Now here comes Bush Jr.
with quazillions in his treasure chest
he bought himself an election, honey
money beats out all the rest

Dubya assured himself a position
as our titular head
and many a would be voter will watch
the election results at home in bed

for no matter how hard
his opponent may run
we all know Bush Jr.
this race has won

now don't you dare say
that I am crass, cynical, or snide
if the election process really worked
it would fill me with pride

please read my lips, I must reiterate
you see, it isn't just a joke
Ron Reagun became president
Before I got to vote.

(Feb. 1991

Little Tommy Jefferson

We were declared Independent...
by our country's Fathers...
Declared independent of the...
Declaration of Independence
Needing no help from them

Snatched from our families' arms
brought to a foreign land
molested and raped by the fathers
of America who declared
their rights to be self evident

We hold these truths to be self evident
that all...
We hold some truths to be self evident
That some...
men are equal, some men are free

we declare that little Tommy Jefferson
stole the words he said...
From Thomas Paynes' famous pamphlet...
Changing the meaning not to include everyone
Making all basic rights only for some...

That we are endowed by our Creator
With certain inalienable rights...

The right to rape babies...
The black half sister of your wife...
Molest and mistreat her
And still be called mister
If you are little Tommy Jefferson

Now it is known that the mighty member of
the Secret Order of the Mason's,
the Illuminati was a man who
talked white
and slept black.

Kidnapping Sally Hemings in the night
Taking her to another country
Cause that's all right
If you are a father
of the country of America

declaring your rights
to say and do as you please
making rules as you go
cause you're a Mason with Degrees
sleeping black and talking white

little Tommie Jefferson
so worried about blood quantum
and one drop of black blood
let his farm and his business
fall into the mud

That among these rights
are the rights to life
as a 1/16, 1/32/,1/64
quadroon, octoroon, baboon
created by the macaroon, little Tommie Jefferson

the father of our country
our hero, thief, plagiarizer,
child molester, pedophile,
slave trader all in
the pursuit of his happiness, slept black, talked white

We need to change history
history his story, make it self evident
his story needs to be changed
to her story, my story, our story, everyone's story.
we need a Declaration of Independence.

(1980's)

<u>Liopantimanzelle</u>

Oh King!
Majestic, stately King
There you stand
In all your glory
And royalness
You have forgotten
More history
Then the grave robbers
will ever discover
I am your
Liopantimanzelle
Mate…

Oh rare
Beautiful black racer
Running through
Our hearts, our minds
Your blackness so
Much a part of you
Exuding from every
Fiber of you
I am your
Liopantimanzelle
Mate…

Oh provider
Lover of family
Keeper of territories
Conqueror of the unjust
A breed so rare
An entity almost extinct
Teaching us all

To be loyal and true
Loving you is easy to do
I am your
Liopantimanzelle
Mate...

Oh intellect
Scientist, mathematician
Physician to the world
Politician, architect, statesman
All physical and mental
Combined to create
A perfect specimen
A design supreme
For all humankind
I am your
Liopantimanzelle
Mate...

Oh rarity
Endangered species
I've heard so much
About your kind
Been fooled by those
Who look like you
Try to be you
Could never be you
I am your
Liopantimanzelle
Mate

Oh glory
Could it be I found you
I've seen you

from a distance
and I want you
not to cage you
not to enslave you
we're each others
missing parts
I am your
Liopantimanzelle
Mate.

(1960's and constantly revised)

**Lio-pan-ti-man-zelle (a word coined by Xennia Gittoes-Singh)*

Live the Dream

Our hero's always knew
No rights supersede human rights

No man is worse than you are
No man is less or beneath you

No man is better than you are
No man is greater or above you

Your rights begin exactly
where mine end

We are free to
Live the dream

Harriet Tubman dreamt
she could walk to freedom

She made herself
and others free

live
the dream

Frederick Douglas
dreamt he could read

He earned 17 PHDs
Now we all can learn to read

We
live the dream

The Wright brothers dreamed
they could fly in the sky

Mr. Ford dreamed
He could have a horseless ride

Now we fly in the planes
And we drive our cars

We
live the dream

Nelson Mandela dreamed
he could free his people's country

after 26 years in prison
he was the leader of all of South Africa

We saw him
live the dream

Thurgood Marshall dreamed all men
Could be treated fairly in America

He was elected to the Supreme Court
And he made a real difference

Langston Hughes, the great poet
Dreamed of America

"Dream of my dreams," he said
"I am America

I am America, seeking the stars
America."

Students we now
Live the dream

Martin Luther King Jr. dreamed one day
All children could get along

People could all work together
Live together, play together

We
live the dream

Lets celebrate that our heros
dared to Live the dream

lets honor them by
doing the same

some say anything a man can dream
a man can do

lets dream of great things
then carry out our dreams

so one day our children
will see us as hero's

and they too can
live the dream

live the dream
live the dream !

(written for Lorne Magnet School 1999)

Part II

My White Skinned Friend's
Poems on Racism
for the 21st Century

An Anthology

Edited by

XENNIA GITTOES-SINGH
A.K.A. ~~~Running Waters~~~

This anthology is an offering to help prove Einstein's' theory that there is no such thing as race.

Einstein's theory "All modern people are the conglomeration of so many ethnic mixtures that no pure race remains.... It is impossible for any individual to trace every drop of blood in his constitution... After we go back a few generations our ancestors increase so prodigiously that it is practically impossible to determine exactly the various elements which constitute our being."

Acknowledgments

This anthology came about because of many people to whom I would like to give thanks and props :

First, all glory to my deceased birth mother Edith JoNeil Gaddy who made me intensely interested in who I am and how I fit in the world. Edie loved being a black woman. She was a self- taught sixth grade dropout who graduated from nursing school at 60 yrs. old. She was an avid reader and she made me interested in civics, politics, and knowledge of every kind.

To my mentor and eighth grade teacher the deceased Honorable Mayor Everette Lattimore from Plainfield, New Jersey who taught me to love Black History and myself. I called Mr. Lattimore years after junior high school. Just one day out of the blue I decided to call his office. The Union County Comptroller took my call right away. When I told him that I wanted to learn how to go about getting into college he said he would stop what he was doing, pick me up and personally take me to college to make sure I got a good start. He introduced me to Mr. Pryor who helped mentor me through Union College. I earned a six year scholastic scholarship to Fordham University but turned it down because I would be too far from my three children during the day. I graduated from Seton Hall University. Years later, on a whim again, I called Mr. Lattimore while he was Mayor of Plainfield. He wrote a glowing reference letter to Bristol Myers Squibb that was responsible for helping me to score a shot at a corporate career. I can NEVER thank Mr. Lattimore enough.

To Mr. Garzilla(?) who taught me that I was a writer also in the eighth grade.

To `Uncle Bobby' Larry L. Tucker, deceased Honorary Mayor of Plainfield, N. J. who gave my mother all the collected works of Frederick Douglas for me to read when I was 12 years old. Uncle Bobby fought the good fight and got lots of people to get on the bus for the famous MLK March on Washington. No politician ever tried to do anything in NJ from either party without the nod from Uncle Bobby and that's a fact!

To Mr. Hank Pryor who mentored me through college and submitted my name for the Rhodes Scholarship. Mr. Pryor told me it was an honor to be second among a number of students, to me, it simply means I lost ☺) He recommended me for Who's Who in American Jr. Colleges. Homecoming Queen and placed me on every prestigious college and community board that he could think of. Mr. Pryor you have my deepest appreciation for giving me some feelings of self worth. Years after I graduated my mother was student nursing in a hospital when she met a patient who said he was a dean at Union College. My mother said her daughter had attended the school. (She and I were estranged during my college years). She said my name. She said Mr. Pryor cried. "Tears of happiness," he said. He shared stories of my college adventures with her. I hadn't kept in touch with him. I didn't know he cared so much. About three years later I mentioned his name to my mother and she told me this story. I wanted to contact him, to make up for lost time, but she said he was dead. I cried. She said she didn't know he meant that much to me.

To Deborah Stapleton my Seton Hall University Professor/ Counselor who mentored me through college and impressed me with her knowledge of African American History. Ask Debby a question and she would rattle off an answer then turn around and write on the blackboard ten or twenty references and authors off the top of her head. It was impressive. We would try to come up with things that would floor her but we never could do it. She inspired me to try to be just like her and prove everything that I say. She is the Professors Professor.

To Robert Burtis Blair my deceased brother who told me that I was blacker than black to white people but not black enough for the black ones...Bobby called himself a revolutionary. He convinced a lot of people to believe the things he said and the way he lived. In the late 1960's, early `70's my brother said that race issues were ploys used by the 1% to keep poor people fighting each other instead of them. He gathered funding to start the Somerset County Health Clinic in Somerville N. J. that bore his name until the late 1990's.He opened daycare centers, farms in upper NY State, Colorado and North Carolina that sold food through food co-ops. He opened a teaching auto mechanic school and bought housing for the people to share. He fed the poor and homeless for every holiday and started toy drives for the children. He gathered people together of all races, religions, cultures, ages and creeds. My brother was assassinated in1974. They say his neighbor and good friend for years (who was a good Catholic Puerto Rican whom Bobby had just given the deed and keys to a new residence and record store) went to his auto, got a gun and shot my brother in the head and then shot himself.

Three guns were found on the scene. No professional courtesy was extended to our police chief brother from Michigan when he approached the Somerset County police to investigate our brothers' death. Bobby this collection is for you.

To my brother, the Honorable Gary L. Loster who NEVER used his race as an excuse and became one of the first frogmen in the marine corps special forces. Then became the youngest and first black Chief of Police in Saginaw, Michigan. He traded that position to become the first black Chief of Security for General Motors, a Seventh Day Adventist Minister and the Mayor of Saginaw who works tirelessly to unite Africa with American technology and economics.

To my blood brothers Steven Gaddy (living in North Carolina) Desragh, Narajahn from Chicago Ill. and Rahnjeet from LA, Ca. (Rahnjeet begged me not to publish this book for fear someone would hurt me because of the subject),my step brother Hussein and my sisters Pamela Davidson from East Orange, NJ, Pamela Griffin(did ya' notice I have two sisters named Pam? ☺) and Carlotta Singh from Chicago, Ill. A shout out to my family and friends who would be really angry if I didn't mention them in this book.

To my husband William (Bill) Long for having patience with me while I sweated over this book. Nicole Tucker, my daughter for insisting I write these volumes. To Derek Tucker for being my son.

To Carolyn (Aunt Sissy) Duke from NY, NY who makes everyone she meets read and more importantly buy every word I write. Thank you Aunt Sissy and your neighbors (across the street from Minton's Playhouse- hey girlfriends) and friends for letting me read my poetry in the joints in Harlem during the early 1970's long before anyone else ever imagined it would be the popular thing to do.

To Bristol Myers Squibb the Fortune 5 Corporation as they like to call themselves for teaching me that the good `ole boy system is well entrenched. Never take a job that hires you to fulfill quotas regardless of what you are promised.

To the Los Angeles Cultural Affairs Department for turning down my request for a grant to promote this book because in their exalted opinion the subject of racism is not "socially relevant." Ouch! You didn't have to be so mean about it, you could have just said "no."

To Geneffa Jonker, Laurie Deegan, Tasha and Reggie Wilkins and the other members of the Phillips Institutes Symposium on Racism for suggesting that the Los Angeles Cultural Affairs was wrong and that I should just do this project myself regardless of money or grants.

To my white skinned friends who are truly color-blind and submitted their unique pieces for this book for LOVE.

To the Great Spirit who is LOVE.

And finally, (Whew…) to YOU the reader…without YOU this book is meaningless.

INTRODUCTION

I met my friend Xennia many moons ago. From day one she was like family. She is spirit kin to me, a tie stronger than blood. When she approached me about writing an introduction to this most sensitive work, I was honored and of course flattered but secretly pleased.

Xennia works very hard to create harmony in a world we are told is full of dysfunction. This woman, this poet, this friend has not led the easiest of lives, yet her approach to life is one of love without cliché. And her concept for this anthology, that of exchanging viewpoints on race from some of her rather paler friends is nothing short of brilliant and furthers her cause.

Life is a matter of viewpoints that we exchange; some are individual P.O.V.'s (points of view), some are shared, some are catered to and some just lie down and die or cause others to die.

In this precious volume, that you hold in your hands lies the secrets of the universe, poets doing what they do best writing poems to create a better world, or shock people out of indifference, and then smiling upon one another.

Larry Jaffe

Note from the editor,

I have been a spoken word artist in Los Angeles, Ca. for a few years and I had heard many wonderful poems about racism from many people. I thought it would be a good idea to have my white skinned friends share their poems on racism with anyone who would be interested in helping to eradicate racism. I realize there is no such word as white skinned however for purposes of this anthology I wished to use this term because it it definitive.

I agree with our late great Supreme Court Justice Thurgood Marshall's statement, when he was asked on the occasion of his retiring from his position in the court, if he would like to see a black man replace him. Justice Marshall said, "All people with black skin ain't black." The Justice was correct. His statement can be said for white skin people as well as black.

I believe communication is a partial solution to problem solving it isn't the only answer but it is a good start. I hope this anthology stimulates discussion.

I simply put the call out for poems on this subject with no format, no agenda, no preconceived ideas...and glory, they came...this book is a manifestation of that wish ...my editing consisted of trying to place the poems I received in some kind of "categories" (yuck, I hate that word), and correct any typos. Any emphasis placed on words in the various poems are the authors alone.

I pray this collection will be a small step toward peace, harmony and love for my ancestors and perhaps humbly one day the rest of mankind.

Love,
Xennia Gittoes-Singh
A.K.A ~~~Running Waters~~~

PLACES

Can it be that there are still places in America where one person can feel superior to another because of skintone, religion, sex, or sexual preference? Has Southern Hospitality changed to include everyone or are there still places in the south and elsewhere where you can't go in there? Has the KKK Diminishing Muster? Do we still have to be one Exact Shade to matter? "Hey, it's just a game," you say, "Racism is a figment of your vivid imagination. Get that chip off your shoulder there are only Isolated Incidents." Do those places still exist here in 21st century America?

~~~Running Waters ~~~

Southern Hospitality

by Michael Grover

(1)
My mother was born in Georgia
Under confederate flag blankets.
Racism burning in the soul of the south,
Like a cross and white sheets in the front yard.

(2)
I remember visiting her cousin in South Carolina.
He lived in a modest house on the edge
Of a large tobacco field.
Looking on to the field you could see
The workers were all dark,
Skin gleaming with sweat
Of a mid-July heat
Looking beyond the field you could see the
Plywood shacks, this was called home.
You could see their children working beside them,
That's called edjucation.
I remember we were all talking outside,
And a man walked in from the field
With an empty water cooler.
I guess my mothers cousin wanted to show off,
He wanted to show us what a big man he was.
He looked at that black man,
And he said "Boy . . ."
The black man turned obediently.
"How many times have I told you
to use the back door, boy?' He said.
After all that I had witnessed
My opinion shrunk of him yet more.

I actually smiled when that man
Died of a heart attack.

(3)
I'm all grown now,
And I have a life of my own
Far away from the south,
And all of it's deep rooted hate.
I have learned to be my own man.
My mother still lives in the south,
South Florida that is.
I wonder if my lover and I
Were to give her grandchildren
And they were to come out the wrong color.
I wonder if the word niggers would escape her lips
As quickly as it did on my lover.

can't go in there

by Larry Jaffe

you can't go in there
the sign said
colored only
no whites allowed
you can't go in there son
the gas station attendant
rubbed me the wrong way
with his gaze and words
and attitude
you can't go in there boy
the one you want is over
there he pointed with
drool and grease encrusted finger
i looked up at him
with new man's eyes
of teenage assertion
knowing i had just
became a man
in god's eyes
freshly bar mitzvahed
you can't go in there boy
the sign said
colored only
no whites allowed
i just need to pee
i muttered
under my breath
i just need to pee
and really did not care
what the damn sign said
never having seen

such scenic revulsion before
living in my savant suburban cocoon
all these years
you can't go in there boy
i am not a boy
i am a man now
i can go anywhere i want
i thought to myself
as redneck poster boy
started getting to me
at the beginning of my manhood
and betraying confidence
i did not have
i just need to pee
i said a little louder
you can't go in there
the sign said
colored only
no whites allowed
i went in anyway
looked like every
gas station restroom
i had ever seen before or since
and except for the sign
it was no different
sink
toilet
urinal
and despite what the sign said
the fixtures were all white
and none colored
mystified i took a leak
in off-white porcelain
taking hold of

jewish circumcised self
holocaust rhythms
lambasting my soul
thinking thoughts of
redneck euphoria
humming the chorus to
if they could see me now
i took a leak anyway
even though the sign
said colored only
i did not go up in a puff of smoke
i did not come down with some
rare infectious disease
i did wash my hands though
and no color rubbed off onto my fingers
you can't go in there
the sign said
colored only
no whites allowed
i went in there
wondering what the sign really meant
i came out of there
knowing i would always go in there
and even though such signs appear to be down
they are still up in such minds
but i will always go in there
i will always go in there

Diminishing Muster

by CaLokie

There had been ten going out to dine;
One choked himself, and there were nine.
The surviving nine sat up very late;
When one overslept, there were eight.
The eight remaining traveled to Devon;
One said he'd stay there; then there were seven.
The seven continuing chopped up sticks;
One chopped himself in half then there were six.
Six survivors played with a hive;
A bumble bee stung one; now there were five.
The five left decided to go in for law:
One got in chancery and then there were four.
The three persevering went to a zoo;
A big bear hugged one; then there were two.
There was now only two left sitting in the sun.
One got frizzled up, and then there was one. . . .

The title of this paraphrased ditty is "Ten Little Nigger Boys" It was one of 800 rhymes collected by Iona and Peter Opie for the Oxford Nursery Rhyme Book published in New York in 1955.
In their preface they single out this poem along with "The Twelve Days of Christmas" as the fun children can have while learning with counting rhymes.

"The diminishing muster of 'Ten Little Nigger Boys' and the increasing munificence of the gifts presented during the 'Twelve Days of Christmas,'" they point out, "may be confirmed by the mathematically minded."

How was the finalist diminished. . . ? Oh, yes, we still have one, don't we?
"One little nigger boy living all alone;
He got married, and then there were none."

A different final solution to this subtracting song also came out in 1955.
A "little nigger boy" from Chicago visiting his grandfather in Mississippi,
said, "Bye, Baby" to a redneck's wife as he left a country grocery store.
It would've been better for him to have uttered the name of the Lord in vain. . .

His mutilated body was found a week later in the Tallahatchie River
and sent back north where Emmett Till's mother had an open casket funeral
to let the world see what they had done to her only child.

Exact Shade

by Katie O'Loughlin

Race in America
white man black man
different separate
and I learned I am part of white man
separate part of a different race
in America, to someone black, I am part of the white man
in America, to someone white, I am part of the white man
and in America this is to have blood on your hands
a long history of blood on your hands
no real way to remove it
and certainly there would be no real way to remove it now
when there is still such division derision
the wounds not healed
the problem not solved
to be black in America, is
to not be treated fairly
to not get a cab
to not be selected for a house, a job
to be thought a potential criminal
to be thought less of
you must overcome
you must shout your pride
you must fight and struggle to gain an equal life
which comes so much easier when you are white

in America I am part of the white man
but my history, my family is from Ireland

I was raised Irish
Erin go braugh and Ireland forever

and my people my history that I was taught
is surviving the potato famine
when the British were shipping food away from Ireland
as over a million Irish starved to death in shacks and in fields
subjugated religion taken away
language taken away
power taken away
food warmth means for survival
so easily so often taken away
we arose
the poor the masses arose
by the rising of the moon
by the rising of the moon
there then it was British oppressing subjugating
the Irish
and then Protestants with the power against the Catholics
my family was Irish and my family was Catholic
and my name would have told you this
and my voice would have told you this
and my family came to the promised land
and here in America
my family is white I am white

we, the fighters of oppression
we who were forced to learn, hidden in hedge schools,
when teaching a Catholic was illegal
the survivors of the famine
the survivors of the crown ruling the land,
taking the food, the farms
and here we are white I am white

my sister Geri got married to a British man
and my Irish nana, stuck in old times
came to the wedding

saying to the family about my sister and her British groom
"sometimes these mixed marriages work"
what is your dividing line
where do you divide
"sometimes these mixed marriages work"

in America I am white
we have divided by skin color
and so I am white
part of white and separate from black

my good friend is black
and so I am separate from her
I cannot know what it is like to often be
the only black person in a room in a country
where this is ultimately important
I cannot know what it is like to be a young black girl growing up
watching television where all of the families were white
where all of the Barbies were white
and where Little Red Riding Hood, Cinderella, Goldilocks and Snow White
were all white
what is it like to not see your color in stories?

I am white
I live in a country where I am separate solely because my skin is a
different shade
light to black
light to black
skin a different color
where does it separate
where is the exact shade that crosses the line

that makes you different separate divided

America is a mixing pot
in America so much black mixed in with white
so much white mixed in with black
where is the shade
where is the exact shade
where someone becomes different separate divided

I have a friend who is Irish, Native American, Indian and African American
and she is called black

I have a friend who was born in Vietnam to a French Cambodian Vietnamese
mother
and a Spanish North African father
and was raised in America by white parents since the age of two
and he is called   simply   black

I have a good friend whose creative painter father was African American and
Cherokee
and whose artistic loving mother's ancestry is Swiss
she is called simply black
where is the rest of her history
where is the rest of all of who she is
in that word
that description   black

America is a melting pot
but we separate divide de-unify
black white different
black white

black against white
white against black
why

I dated, cared for, a man
and his deep dark skin looked so beautiful
against my pale body
black against white
white against black
is there a shade that makes me
different separate divided
I do not believe it exists
I do not believe I am so very separate
my good friend is black and she makes my life a joy
black white white black
I'm wondering where is the exact shade where I am supposed to be different
from someone
separate from someone
where is it
why do people believe it exists
why are we still asking questions about color
so many years
and we are still living bound up by differences in mere color
as if this separates and divides us
as if all of our differences aren't why our world is so beautiful
everyone unique collectively a melting pot
a multi cultural
smorgasbord of colors sizes voices songs histories knowledge ideas
no one can make me believe that there is a shade that divides me from

another
that there is a point at which I am to believe I am divided from another
a multicultural smorgasbord of colors sizes voices songs histories
knowledge
ideas

I am a piece of all of this
I am a part of all of this
I am tall and Irish and I sing and I write and I have long hair
and full hips and pale skin dotted with many many freckles
and I am kind and honest and I love to garden and cook
and I am hetro and liberal and I love red, intense bright blue
and gadgets and I love to run and I dislike bright lights
and I have been many places
and I have many stories

and all these things I bring
all these things I bring as my part in the multicultural, melting pot lives we are living
we all bring so many different things
shades of this and shades of that
in America we use words that are so limiting
black white black white
we all bring so many different things

C Katie O'Loughlin 2000

hey it's just a game

by Larry Jaffe

so i am rooting
for the home team
my team
i pledge
allegiance to
the flag of the united
states of sports
statistics and suburbia
i'm rooting for my team
my home team
the new york jews
or the ny kikes as
they are fondly known
but yesterday some
native hebrews
came running out
to protest the game
they claimed we
were stealing their
heritage and mocking
their name
just because
our mascot
runs around the
field in native hebrew garb
you know he has those
cute spit curls on the side
of his head
and he wears one of
those yarmulke things
a beany on his head

and one of their prayer shawls
it's supposed to be
authentic so i don't
really know what their problem
is after all it's just a game
and we make sure
that when we are rooting
for the team that we
use all the proper
gestures in the stands
many of us have even practiced
like we copied our shoulder
shrugs from
vaudeville acts they
show on the big screen
and when the whole
crowd shouts OY
it is enough to raise
the hairs on the back
of your head
and when we chant
shalom when the
team is up to bat
well we just seem
undefeatable somehow
and well we
even know how
to do that little dance
jews are known to do
at weddings and such
we are very authentic
you know
and hava nagilla
is a great tune

we sing it and dance it
in the stadium
thousands of us doing
it together
especially when our rabbi mascot
goes into his prayer dance
out in the bleachers
he looks so real
he looks so jewish
you would never know he is not
i think they use makeup
to get that effect
or maybe he wears one
of those life masks
molded off a real rabbi
to get that effect
all i know is that he
really knows how
to get the crowd going
with his prayers and stuff
i heard next year
they may get another
guy out there with him
who can sing
they call him
a cantor or something
i think because of
eddie cantor
a dead jewish singer guy
i mean i don't know what
these hebrews are
complaining about
i think we are honoring them
and paying tribute

to them when our little jews
are running the base paths
and we cheer them on
screaming la chaim
another quaint jewish
authentic saying
at the top of our lungs
personally i think it is
really picky of them
to object
i mean the mascot
and the team logo
look so authentic
we took careful
pains to not be
offensive and be
politically correct
you know
we did not make
the nose on the mascot
rabbi's face too big
did not want to be
objectionable
otherwise no one
would come out to
the game

Isolated Incidents

by CaLokie

President Clinton called the killing of [James] Byrd shocking and outrageous.
He said the residents here "must join together across racial lines to demonstrate that an act of evil like this is not what this country is all about." Carol Marie Cropper, June 11, 1998, New York Times

Isolated 1998 incident near Jasper, Texas where a 49-year-old black man with a crippled left hand, after beaten by three white supremacists, is dragged by a chain from the back of a pickup truck for 2 1/2 miles
his body disintegrating into 75 pieces--his head and arm found a mile from his torso. . .
not to be confused with

isolated 1998 incident before Wyoming ranch
where gay university student Matthew Shepard was lashed to split wooden rails of a fence post, tortured with cigarette burns, pistol-whipped and left to die in near-freezing temperatures. . .
not to be confused with

isolated 1999 incident in northern suburbs of Chicago
where 21-year-old white supremacist in blue car prowling the streets for Jews, blacks and Asians shoots and kills African-American father walking with his daughter and son and then Korean graduate
student as he entered a church . . .
not to be confused with

isolated 1995 incident near Fort Bragg, North Carolina

where 3 skinhead soldiers from the 82nd Airborne Division looking for a black person in a dimly lit area with a 9 mm, spot a black couple walking and murder them. . .
not to be confused with

isolated 1984 incident in Denver where a terrorist gang known as the Silent Brotherhood shot and killed Jewish radio talk-show host Alan Berg. . .
not to be confused with

isolated 1997 incident in Denver, Colorado
where a 19-year-old neo-nazi using a .22-caliber pistol
executes a West African man at a bus stop because
he thought he didn't belong there. . .
not to be confused with

isolated 1984 incident on New York subway
where a white vigilante shot four black youths
who had asked him for money, paralyzing one. . .
not to be confused with

isolated 1992 incident at a Brooklyn station house
where cops rammed a stick into the rectum
of Albert Louima, a Haitian immigrant. . .
not to be confused with

isolated 1986 incident in New York neighborhood of Howard Beach, where a dozen young white males find three young men eating pizza guilty of being black and pursue them with tree limbs, bricks, baseball bats. . .chase
one onto the Belt Parkway,
where he was killed by a car. . .
not to be confused with

isolated 1921 incident in Tulsa, Oklahoma
where a white mob frustrated in their attempt to lynch
a single black man, riot and kill approximately 300 blacks...
not to be confused with

isolated 1992 incident in Los Angeles
where violence and fires erupted after 4 police officers
were acquitted by a nearly all-white Simi Valley jury who saw
nothing wrong in the way Rodney King was whacked . .
not to be confused with

isolated 1955 incident in Mississippi
where a white jury acquitted two rednecks
of their torture murder of Emmett Till. . .
not to be confused with

isolated incident two years before the coming century
and millennium near Jasper, Texas. . .

not to be confused withTHIS IS NOT WHAT AMERICA'S ALL ABOUTisolated incident
not to be confused withTHIS IS NOT WHAT AMERICA'S ALL ABOUTisolated incident
not to be confused withTHIS IS NOT WHAT AMERICA'S ALL ABOUTisolated incident
not to be confused withTHIS IS NOT WHAT AMERICA'S ALL ABOUTisolated incident
not to be confused withTHIS IS NOT WHAT AMERICA'S ALL ABOUTisolated incident
not to be confused withTHIS IS NOT WHAT AMERICA'S ALL ABOUTisolated
incident

PEOPLE / INFLUENCES

"People, people who need people…"
live in COMMUNE ities
NEIGHBOR hoods
RESIDENT al areas
Living with or near each other
Seeking their fellow man out for approval
Influencing behavior and thought …
Sometimes sending Christmas Cards in January forgetting that it just might take 41 bullets to kill a man armed with a wallet
People like Johnny Rocker, yes even our Grandmother may not know what The Truth is…or why people will still write an Ode to Veronica or appreciate A Blues and Gospel Collaboration and sing a Song for Mumia or love the ballet of a beautiful Hoopster because they just can't understand that people really need and influence …people.

~~~Running Waters~~~

Christmas Card in January

by Stazja McFadyen

Miguel came north
across the Rio Grande
asking permission from no one
except his wife who stayed behind
to care for an infant and elderly kin.

Too far, too expensive. too risky
to travel home for Christmas,
he came to his boss's house for dinner,
outshone the glittery decorations
proudly passing his family snapshots
around the table.

With rugged workman's hands
he lifted the boss's
fair haired grandboy
like a nativity gift
and crooned the Spanish carol
he would sing to his own son next year.
The boss's wife and daughter
offered him second helpings
of everything.

He apologized in broken English
"have not good words enough
to say my heart."
Moist gratitude in peaceful eyes
spoke eloquent volumes.

The boss's teenage son was on
the work crew in July the day

officials stopped the company pick up,
identified Miguel by name
and took him away.
At home that night the boss's son,
a boy-now-man,
wept without shame in the telling.
An envelope postmarked Mexico
arrived the following January.
A christmas card, on the outside
a snow-covered house
billowing smoke from the chimney
depicted the unseen warmth within,
a message from Miguel
in artisan's elegant penmanship
remembering with love
his friends in Texas.

41 bullets

by CaLokie

"Stop-them-all" New York Mayor and Police
Commissioner tell Street Crimes Unit
The vast majority of people stopped
by these cops are Black or Latino
41 bullets
four officers
one man dead

SCU motto becomes "We Own the Night"
Crime in New York City cut in half
Claims of police misconduct rise 45%
payments by city in those cases rise 38%
41 bullets
four officers
one man dead

Around midnight plainclothes police quartet
in unmarked patrol car cruise "no man's land"
Amadou Diallo, 22-year-old street vendor,
returns to Bronx borough apartment
41 bullets
four officers
one man dead

They're on "field inspection" to make arrests
and turn up information about rapist in area
Amadou discusses electric bill with roommate
and then goes out for something to eat
41 bullets
four officers
one man dead

Driving on Wheeler Avenue, they spot black man
acting suspiciously
Relatives and neighbors describe Diallo as shy,
devout Muslim who didn't smoke or drink
41 bullets
four officers
one man dead

They approach suspect standing in vestibule
Suddenly he reaches for gun. . . .
Four men in ties with guns get out of car
he reaches for wallet. .
41 bullets
four officers
one man dead

From Bronx to upstate county in New York, where 86%
of population is white, 9% black, moves trial of--
From Kennedy Airport to West African nation
of Guinea flies body riddled by fusillade of--
41 bullets
four officers
one man dead

Putting themselves in place of police fearing death
that night, 8 white 4 black Albany jury acquit--
Knowing it could've been them, demonstrators
before spot where Diallo was shot protest--
41 bullets
four officers
one man dead

JOHNNY ROCKER

by Don "Kingfisher" Campbell

Whiteboy
Wants to solve the problems of the world
Whiteboy
Puts colored people in prison
Whiteboy
Doesn't give jobs to anyone who looks different
Whiteboy
Lets minorities study 30 yr. old textbooks in carpetless schools
Whiteboy
Sell toys priced just high enough to maintain the divide
Whiteboy
Drags old prejudices out from his father's mouth
Whiteboy
Wishes to bring back the 50s when everyone knew their place
Whiteboy
Needs an education
Whiteboy
Must be taught using his methods
Don't blame us
Whiteboy
If we're violent
Don't blame us
Whiteboy
If we're not fair
Whiteboy
We've learned so much on how to dominate the world from you
Whiteboy
Don't you know you're the biggest problem in history

<u>Grandmother</u>

by Deon T. Standlee

I got a new pen and it's not afraid to write
of the horrors that fill our history, <u>my</u> history

Of the cruel treatment of African-Americans
branded with the name "Slave"
because they were a strong and beautiful people
misunderstood by their captors...

Captors, who in another century,
would be looking to them as allies and Holders
of the Original Culture.

My ancestors held slaves.
I don't know how they treated them,
but I have repented of their sins,
because I will not justify the sin
by claiming ignorance of the treatment.

My grandmother speaks of those "mexicans
and nigger children" and I cringe -
feeling that my mere presence in the same
room
with her words will indict me -
as a perpetrator of an oppression
waged, first, by my forefathers.

I sit in this room with the horrible racist statements
flowing out of my grandmother's soul.
and I, too, feel like a slave - bound to a history I cannot
change

These horrors are engraved on the insides of my eyelids and I am unable to turn back time, but I can change the future.

I can speak out truth and reason and equality
And I can cover my grandmother's mouth with my tears
and her words with my compassion
and I can teach her to trust again.

But I will not tolerate her words-
this insistence of innocence (concerning this horror)
these "hands clamped over deaf ears"
to reason and compassion and repentance.

Like Simon Wiesenthal once said,
"Hope lives when people remember."

The Truth is ...

by Stazja McFadyen

Outside the Salvation Army Rehabilitation Center
a boy of eight or ten,
rich dark skin
the color of fertile silt
along the banks of the Gulf of Guinea
descendent of distant Nigerian Igbo,
a colored boy
stands beside
another smaller colored child
waiting to cross when
rush hour traffic breaks.

That is the fact
but not the truth,
not the whole truth...

This young boy
being his brother's keeper
holds a loving protective arm
across the chest of restless kid brother
anxious to MOVE

This boy and I make eye contact
and the truth is
he's proud and self contained.

The truth is
unless the circumstances
that landed his family there
at the Salvation Army
break him

by societal contagion
of racial hatred
of poverty-stricken provocation
or outcome-based education
The truth is the beauty
of one young boy
mastering manhood.

(previously published in "Maytag Heights" anthology, Lummox Press, and in the chapbook "Where Would I Be Without You? Love Songs to My Road Atlas")

ODE TO VERONICA

by Ray Badders

This poem is for you, Veronica
I never knew you
I never spoke with you
I knew your name, though
It was Veronica

You were the only colored kid
in the second grade
in my elementary school
in the 50's in Baltimore

You moved away at the end of the year
but I never knew you I never teased you
You were different from Elizabeth
whom I truly loved
You were Veronica

The 50's gave way to the 60's
Up in Baltimore
Kennedy was shot
His brother was killed
And King could no longer dream
Veronica became black and proud

She was now an Afro-American
She wore a 'fro and used a pik.
She listened to soul music.
She ate soul food
And whitey was on the moon.

I left for Nam in '69

I left the hippies
I left the druggies
I left the angry blacks
We found community in the Nam.

That was short lived.
We were surrounded by enemies
The Cong, the hippies, the peacenics
Turned the brothers - in - arms
Into brothers and whites.

Veronica became a soul sister
She hated all that wasn't black
Me, an eighth generation American
The grandson of a German immigrant
The grandson of a Pennsylvania pig farmer
Became the source of Veronica's problems.

Now it's the 80's
Veronica has to make up for lost time.
The dream that died has died hard.
The dreamer was shot on a balcony.

Give way to the new African American
Give way to Veronica
Give way to Sharpton & Jackson & Farrakhan
Get outta the way you Uncle Toms!

Oh Veronica
Where have you been?
Oh Veronica
Where are you going?
Oh Veronica
What are you teaching your children?

Are white kids the devil?
Are they a scientist's mistake?
Are white kids bad seeds?
Are they like you once were, Veronica?

My white kids are the only white kids
in their elementary school
in the new millenium
in the U.S. of A.

El Poemo Negro

by jimmy jazz

I looked down at my shadow
and thought
I was Thelonius Monk
and surmised
that if a piano
suddenly materialized on this rooftop
I could play it
by virtue of a goatee and sunglasses
Then I remembered that cool doesn't cut it

A Blues-Gospel Collaboration

by CaLokie

Fatt-Back bluesman's slide guitar
and Jook Joint crew's harmonica
and drums call African man
and blond European woman
in wheelchair
onto pub parquet floor
where they slowly move around
till the blues raise her
like Jesus did
the paralytic from the pallet
lowered by gospel quartet pals
atop a Capernaum house

The rainbow couple dance
cheek to cheek
chest to breast
waist to waist
leg to leg
through that number
and the next

I leave
As far as I know
she still don't need
that chair

SONG FOR MUMIA

by Steve Baratta

You are not forgotten
In your darkest hour.
You are not alone. We
Who stand for decency
Are still with you.

Prejudice and injustice
Entering a system based on
Justice, equality for all
Only means
The milk of human kindness

Has gone sour. Leaving
A bad taste in the mouths
Of those who do care.
You are not alone.
Let alone forgotten.

If you have wondered
If God had forsaken you?
No. It's only the struggle
Against inhumanity.
A long hard road.

It's a test.
One of endurance
Strength and character.
You will conquer
You have what it takes.

Prejudice and injustice

Entering a system based on
Justice, equality for all
Is a statement of that system
Or society condoning it.

By our constitution.
All men
Are created equal
Or is that,
Created equal biologically?

Hoopster

by Larry Jaffe

It all started on the playground
Shooting hoops with friends
There were five Larry's
In our neighborhood
And when one mama shouted Larry
All five commenced running
This time three waiting
High School bus sojourn
We played horse
A basketball game
Of ghostlike pretensions
Winner takes all
To the next morning contest
We aimed potshots at the basket
Without acclaim a
Time passing ritual
Suddenly
Larry Mohlman shouted
At Larry Kempster
You're just like a Jew
You can only do one thing
Cause he kept shooting lay-ups
And was not basketball worldly and wise
Did not diversify his shots
And kept driving persistence
To the backboard
I looked on in disbelief
Just as suddenly realizing why Molhman
Always picked on me since age of six
So with hook shot in hand
Set shot from perimeter

And jump shot from downtown
This Larry
Meaning Jaffe
Asked that Larry
Meaning Mohlman
If I shot just like a Jew too
He did not answer
Turning red as his hair

As I proceeded to
Take him to the cleaners
While all I could think
About were showers

FEELINGS / POV / MY PERSPECTIVE

Some people hide their feelings very well
Some wear their feelings on their sleeves for all to see
Some see racism
Some see none at all
It all depends on who is doing the looking
we all have a POV (point of view)
about the glass half full
the glass half empty
doesn't matter if we came from Uptown
or way Downtown / Downtown
what matters is Who told you
what, how and when to think as a child
some people are Bigoted about a lot of things
they see Uncle Tom everywhere they go
they laugh at the POV that LOVE is
This Little Package given to us all at birth
Their perspective remains the same even after reading
My Poem on Native Americans After Listening to
John Sinclair Who did Prison Time for Conspiracy
To Destroy Government Property and they still can see no racism
Because they permanently live in
the Dunes of Cerebrum.

~~~Running Waters~~~

Downtown/Downtown

by jimmy jazz

I lost a blues
by singing instead of writing
I had the groove,
but memory has subsided
Alcohol blues
drunk driving and singing blues
We (me and the blues)
were a loud Tom Waits blues
moaning // grunting // ranting
dying inside
in a middle class white-boy kinda way
a happy death
with soft-edge suffering
no serrated-edge rusty-blade
suffering for me
Nigga!

Yeah, I'm talking to you
who has made a choice not to fit in
with the corrupt social order of my majority
my sick old men looking for snuff films
my kiddie porn distribution network
my Xtian fellowship
Remember Patti Smith said,
"Jesus Christ was a nigger,
nigger, nigger, nigger, nigger,
nigger, nigger, nigger."
Say it again and it will lose whatever meaning it has left
She meant "Outside of society" says the professor
same as the confederate Good Ole Boys

and all their inbred klan meant to keep niggers outside of their society
--sheet!
You think "That sounds like racist talk" but don't say anything
Now you think I be thinking I know what it's like to be a black man in
Amerikkka
Well I don't.

part II

He wants to be black
He wants to be black
  because now it's cool
  to be black
Next week he'll be toting
a dashiki to school
  and back
Just to be black
  He likes black music and
he thinks if he was black
music would pour from his poor pores.
He'd sleep with Billie Holiday if
  he was black.
He'd hang out with Panthers and fuck shit up
  if he was black.
He wouldn't never been no slave--
slit the masters throat and teach others
to do the same, while his black nigger body
was swinging from a tree
"the bulging eyes"
"the twisted mouth"
If he was black, he could make extemporaneous speeches

on the way to martyrdom or at least postal stamp visage...
If he was black, women would succumb to his member which would be so big as to need its own membership card at the price
club.
"I be going through 600 condoms a week, if I was black."
He wants to be black
He wants to jump back
in the alley with brother Little Richard and Long Tall Sally
He wants to be black
to get back
to a more natural slack
closer to the earth mother
whose breasts are the rivers
and whose feet are the rich dark roots of trees
He wants to be black
to live in the ghetto with a cadillac
to get back
Jack
to shoot smack
to pimp slap
He wants to be black
He wants to be black

who told you

by Larry Jaffe

who told you that
my jewish nose
was ugly
and deformed
who told you that
who told you that
jews are spawn from
the devil and are
not the chosen people
and who told you
that these jewish noses
are far too big
or our lips way too fat
who told you
was it a message from
your wasp god
who only you
have witnessed
or was it some
beverly hills
plastic psycho surgeon
that makes money
making people
"beautiful"
in someone else's eyes
who told you that it
was okay to be
a bigot
who told you

i will never forget

that time when you
met my dad
and commented
under your breath
after looking at his honker
that now you knew
where my nose got
its brilliant start
you didn't think i heard you
as i let that comment go by
like many others that
are let by
until they turn into
actions that also go by
until it is just too late

so when you look
in the mirror
at that vanilla wasp face
the one lacking definition
and character
staring back at you
do you still think about
how big my nose is
or that my family
was not born on
a golf course
and my last name has
vowels where you
think there should
be consonants
perhaps you should
look into a deeper mirror
and look past

your madras plaid skin
and chameleon
colors that help
you blend into
your society
like homogenized
leather
so worn with
platitudes and lack
of desire
it is a wonder your
race even reproduces
because if your tiny
wasp nose is any reflection
of your anatomy
it is no wonder you
complain about
the length of mine

Bigoted

by CaLokie

You're a nigger
a kike
a wop
a jap
a gook
You're no good
You're no good
You're no good
The only good one of you
is a dead one

You're a bitch
a shrew
a whore
some pussy
a witch
You're no good
You're no good
You're no good
The only good one of you
is a dead one

You're a queer
a sodomizer
a cock sucker
a pervert
a fag
You're no good
You're no good
You're no good
The only good one of you

is a dead one

You're a welfare bum
  a freeloader
  a wino
  a wetback
  a drunkin' injun
You're no good
You're no good
You're no good
The only good one of you
is a dead one

You're a liberal
  an atheist
  a left-winger
  a pinko
  a commie
You're no good
You're no good
You're no good
The only good one of you
is a dead one

UNCLE TOM

by Ray Badders

If I were black
Now that's a hoot

But if I were black
Would I be black enough?
Would I pass the black test?
or would I turn my back on my people?

Would I be an Uncle Tom?
Would I appreciate the dead, white European males
Or would I hold them in distain?

Would I yearn for Mother Africa?
Or would I be content
To live in the land of the free
And the home of the brave?

Who would I be?
Would I be a negro
In the true sense of the word?
Would I be black
And be so hip?
Would I be colored
And pay tribute to my ancestors?
Or would I be modern
And be African-American?
Would I be a nigger
And be worse than bad?
Would I be consumed with my color
And turn it into my god?

Would I find that justice
is color-bound or color-blind?
After all, O.J. can't be guilty
Because he's a strong black man
That the white man is trying to bring down.
If I were a black man
I'd turn my eyes heavenward
And I'd turn my mind to 1863

That's when Abraham Lincoln
A dead white man used by God
In one stroke of the pen
Answered the prayers of my suffering people.

If I were a black man
I'd rejoice in my God and Savior
For letting my people go

I'd turn away from Allah
I'd turn away from Jah
Our people's prayers were answered
by the God of Abraham, Job and Malachi.

If I were a black man
I'd be proud to be called a Tom
For Uncle Tom was humble and peaceful
And placed his faith in Jesus Christ

Jesus Christ, the Son of the living God
The God of Moses
Whose people were enslaved
For sixteen generations

THIS LITTLE PACKAGE

by Deon T. Standlee

I have a little package that I hold within my soul.

It is wrapped like one of my grandmother's valuables
In a plastic bag tied with a rubber band,
Wrapped in a plastic bag tied with a rubber band,
Wrapped in a plastic bag tied with a rubber band.

I open this package carefully and cautiously
For this package holds Anger!
(not just any kind: a special kind)

It's the Anger I unwrap:
When my pride is hurt,
When my family treats me like I am 13 years old,
When my postman won't deliver my mail because
Of my protective dog.

I also unwrap it when men objectify me:
Don't know how to handle my sensuality,
One hand on their manhood and
One hand trying to fondle my sexuality.

I unwrap my Anger to stop my oppression.

This anger was given to me as a gift-
One still under wraps in the hall closet,
Next to the family secrets and skeletons.

It is one gift that has been nourished and fed
For many decades and raised without much light.
It doesn't have eyes to see what I have seen.

It's not surprising that I can't see straight when I unwrap this Anger!

My First Poem on Native Americans, After Listening to John Sinclair, Who Did Prison Time For Conspiracy to Destroy Government Property

by Stazja Mc Fadyen

Marlon Brando and I have more in common
than first meets the eye.
As a black leather jacketed motorcycle hoodlum
in The Wild One, Marlon terrorized a small town.

I wear a tan leather jacket, and sometimes
a three quarter length black leather coat.
Once I rode a black man's Harley,
the freedom wind of the highway whipping my hair.
This would traumatize my mother if I ever told her.

Brando played Kawalski
in "A Streetcar Named Desire."
I'm part Polish; a Pole, not a Polack.
I've walked the French Quarter street of Desire.
Do you begin to see a pattern of similarities
between Marlon Brando and me?

In protest of Native American treatment,
he sent an exotic Apache woman to Hollywood
to decline his Godfather Oscar.

With this poem I withdraw my pledge
to honor a waiver I signed
not to write about the Paiute tribe,
a pledge I made to Richard Bellon,
tribal manager from the Bureau of Indian Affairs,
the agency devoted to keeping
Native Americans ghettoed.

Bellon paid me heap green tax collected wampum
to teach Ft. Bidwell Paiutes how to study.

In their native language, "Geedataku"
means "ground hog eaters."
Dark and greasy stringy meat
main course at a feast
that honored their teacher.

I taught them to study.
They taught me how to side bet
in a cutthroat game of Indian poker,
how to boil red weed into a tea
to ease my menstrual cramps,
how to tell a deer's direction
from hoof prints angles,
taught me thanks for uncontaminated food.

The Paiute hunters thanked their bounty
for its sacrifice.
Their taught their children planting
to replace each Christmas tree they felled
fulfilling their one commercial contract,
a contract Richard Bellon sabotaged,
secretly making a deal that undersold
the Paiute word of honor
for a few dollars more in the tribal coffers.

I took a Sunday walk with Cleavon Phoenix.
Bellon warned me not to socialize with Paiutes.
Richard Bellon never shot hoops
with Cleavon's brother Marvin
but I did. Marvin was a talented artist.
When I arranged Marvin's transport
to college in Oklahoma,

Richard Bellon redisbursed the funds.

No wonder Richard Bellon,
fork-tongued servant for the BA,
inveigled me to keep my own tongue gagged.
This poem could be a crime
but I believe the Paiutes and Marlon Brando,
who knew there is no gain from dehumanizing
their fellow man for a fistful of dollars
would not protest that I break silence.

(previously published in the chap book "Where Would I Be Without You? Love Poems to My Road Atlas")

DUNES OF CEREBRUM

by Jordan Hurder

I am sitting on the couch.
What I'm feeling right now, that's the musical
Mood, played out to a tee
The muse has crept inside my brain
And rattled his ribbed skin against my creative
Console, but as I see these swirling
Images above me
I feel them nipping at my nose when I inhale
The muse denies me the train tracks on which I send
My mental cargo down to the page
So I say FUCK THE MUSE
I'm gonna write, I'm gonna spit my mental
Pops all over and not give
Him the satisfaction of knowing he's
Locked the dunes of cerebrum inside
My head another time
I can't keep going now, I can't
I'll keep going I'm, gonna run
I'm gonna run
What is this a fucking marathon?
Yes, I can see the finish line from here
It's a few lines down
It's the next line down
It's the next line down
Splash Gatorade in my face, man
Splash the regurgitated salt of a neon-green
Creature called mountain misty fruity cum
To give me sustenance
A few lines down
The next line down
Hold a cup of society's woes just under my

Tongue, I lap at it
Fully aware that I'm not just an individual
That I have to take into account the lives and situations
Of all the people on the planet
I exist in the existence of all those who
Define me, I exist as the oppressor
I exist as the subjugated
I exist as the power hungry
I exist as the rich, the poor, the weak, the strong
I exist in a villa and in a toilet
I EXIST IN GUILT and I exist in arrogance
I exist in allsport that tastes like cough syrup
Because U know that all the fresh water that
Could dilute it is starting wars in a region
That my existence oppresses
I won't name it because I exist in that name
And I exist in all the stereotypes that name gives to
The ignorant masses in which yes, unfortunately,
I also exist.
I am sitting on a couch.
I enjoy looking at art, I enjoy listening to music
I am confused.
I'll keep going with disorder to fuel me,
This disorder's become sacred, a beam of light
Reflected off a near star
Off the cornered roof of a house, off a
Mirror laying in the middle of the street
This disorder is a single dab of color
In a famous work of art,
A dab that has smeared with age
Lost its' splendor, taken on a funny smell
A dab that has smeared with age
Lost its splendor, taken on a funny smell
A dab that defines as it defiles

MY EXISTENCE DEFINES AS IT DEFILES

One consonant changes the face of
My existence forever, that change, that
Minute and near-imperceptible star of a change
Is my sacred disorder,
I can't pick a position
I gyrate among options, options that aren't available
Options I haven't discovered yet,
I am the fly in an oldwestern tavern pisspot,
Dodging urine streams for life and I am sacred
I am scarred
I say hello to everything even though I can't
Stop long enough to carry on a conversation
I an not affectionate, but I will reach out
And embrace what passes if it means life or death . . .
I don't want to die because of principle.
I don't want to die because of a belief.
I don't want to die because of a foul smelling dab of
Shit that stains the portrait of my existence.
I want to live because of principle.
I want to live because of my beliefs.
I want to live in the mind of every artist of every poet
Of every novelist of every musician of every
Living thing and encourage nothing more than
The contradictory tapestry we call LIFE*!*
I am sitting on my couch.
The festival rages on around me.
The smells intoxicate.
The liquors make me have to piss so bad that I cross my legs,
Not content even to miss a thing
The people have become one swirling mass
A mass with whom I am hopelessly in love
I can't read the numbers on my watchface, I'm too drunk

Or too excited
Or too inspired (hooray! Fuck you again muse!)
Disregarding the time, in I plunge, taking all of
Society's woes with me
Fleshing out the viewpoints of those who have been silenced
I would like to take tine in this swirling mass
Of people, of ides, of satyrs with thirteen, fifteen, twenty-one inch hard cocks
Who don't make the least attempt to hide them
Of masked dancers who smell of sex, dirty sex, ugly
Violent sex
This chorus of yellow faced singers
I would like to take time before this poem's conclusion
To allow any voice to shape it's direction
To let any voice ring true and fuck the muse
In my head over and over again . . .
(be heard, now is your chance, be heard!)
I am sitting on a couch.
It's late.
I'm tired.
The color I see is red, pierced with orange, blue.
White skin.
The smell I smell is rather foul.
I am at the end of my rope.
I am steadying myself on a million different courses.
My eyes hurt.
Tell me I am important to you even when I'm not around
Because I'll hear it, I'll drink it in my juice
I'll sleep with it in my bed
I'll know it, because my existence will let it in
With it's lifelike open arms.
My brain is tired, it will sleep now.
I am tired, and I thank everyone

PERSONAL / TESTIMONIES

I can personally testify that The Walls can close in on us all if we continue to place ourselves in little Boxes with no Insight: A Disparate Image one to another. Wake up, Americans or they will roll out the Cattle Cars once again At Midnight and in the broad daylight and herd us like Sheep and Goats into their concentration camp jails unless we communicate our true feelings with our fellow man. All of us can stand by hopelessly with Hands Red. Hands Red with the blood of our silence if we don't completely and efficiently eradicate racism and it's vestiges once and for all and give and accept each others heartfelt Apology.

~~~Running Waters~~~

The Walls

by marion k.

Pickets pay no mind during weekday release.
Legally on the ground,
he walks away with 50 bucks
& a fair voucher
in second hand pockets. ~
First expenses: an jalapeno burger instead of chow
& sunmart beer instead of chalk.a smoke.
In La Libre, he leaves:
jigger holdin' to road dogs;
writ writing to in-house lawyers;
& gunning down to snipers
who see through the turnkey's kill shield.
Hearty October afternoon, big
& bright, without a cloud 'cross Texas.
Here, near the forest's perimeter,
Pine trees pine
& Mockingbirds mock.
Skies seems newer
& somehow bluer.
Free air lacks staleness of men.
"What a good day to hold an aggie."
But no! No mas!
"No more hoe squad
& high riding bosses!"
He repeats inside his brain:
"What a good day! What a good day!"
& reciprocates 11th Street "traffic":
white cars with blue seals,
workers driving in gray,
pick-ups of co-eds,
& surely, rumbling chain buses.

My current expedition's tacky labels
("God listens"
&
"MY CHILD IS A LINCOLN HONOR STUDENT")
secure. He walks in front of me
compelling a shift.
Without human assumption,
I murmur my epithets.
Unquestionably,
I am better.
White, church women never get caught.

Boxes

by Jordan Hurder

This is easy I say to myself as I check the caucasian box
Wait a minute didn't I hear a poem about boxes one time
Didn't I read a stack of books about boxes one time
Didn't someone say to me that the intersection of their gender and their race is totally overlooked by the boxes
Didn't someone say that they didn't feel like a person after checking the boxes
Why is it so easy for me?
Oh that's right I'm this country's golden boy, still young enough to kill
Man enough to kill man enough to vote republican
My balls are big and white enough to sit down and shut up
And they reward me with such an easy box no pesky backgrounds to choose from
No heritage's necessarily excluded by simple white me
"don't have a heart don't be conscious and your application for anyfuckingthing will be nice and easy"
I want more boxes yes I do
I want to be white and pissed off
I want to be white and socially liberal and ready to tear down this system
I want a fucking octagon of options I want to check the I'm caucasion but distressed with the term because in general I'm not a big fan of terms boxes
I guess that makes me an other
But my skin is too white no it's true I'm caucasian and there's not a damn thing I can do about it
The life I live encourages me to silence my rage

The life I live encourages me to live with impotent discontent lest I forego all the advantages so benevolently bestowed upon me
I want to understand experiences I've never had
didn't someone once write somewhere that they didn't feel like a person after checking the boxes
Nice and square (and white in the middle) you tell me that it is just my imagination
My white harmless imagination knows no bounds it will break you

Insight: A Disparate Image
by Jerry Hoff

As endorphines soothe
sweat-soaked agitation,
my jaw unclenches
and I lean back, relaxed
into the effort, while
dark green odors rise
oxygen rich
from back of the pond.
Spongy springs unwind
across the path
and mud splatters
moisture-wicking socks,
even in dry weather.

The stocky old man I am--
complete with freckles, wrinkles,
and age-spots--I see
in the eyes of passing children
and smile aloud
at their brassy assumptions.
My tall black friend
jogging with me--
who has perfected the art
of dignified gentling--laughs too
as our greetings
ricochet off concrete faces
set in neutral.
My amusement is at
the recognition
of too many cop shows
in white-face--uptight
parental control.

His laughter, different.

cattle car

by Larry Jaffe

i cannot see myself
boarding a train to
oblivion
a rail to nowhere
i just cannot see myself
going along with the herd
for a ride
i just cannot see myself
despite my jewishness
going into a cattle car
under anyone's volition
let alone my own
you see i just cannot see
myself riding the rails of
a cattle car
or packed inside like human
sardines and someone else
is holding the keys to my future

no i cannot see myself
climbing into the car
or letting my family
climb in this car
without a fight
i would be dead
first
drinking first blood
and i would take some
with me first
cause i don't plan on
moving in with sheep

i would kill my family
and myself first
rather than suffer the
dishonor of mental
dismemberment
you see number tattoos
are not rosebuds or nametags
some say you were not there
i say i was and am reborn yet again
i see disheveled disoriented
jews going for a ride
one way tickets clutched in
hands not made of fists
as they make travel plans to
aushwitz or buchenwalder
i wonder about the travel agent
that sold them these tickets
and the tour guide from hell
that gave them the ride
i wonder who was the father
that took his savings in
exchange for freedom
i cannot see vacationing
in poland as a holiday
this was not noah's ark this was
hitler's ark
nazi's ark
and they were not taking two of
every species
they were taking six million of one
but i cannot see myself doing this
i cannot see myself walking calmly
without a fight
relocation

or death
slowly to holocaust away
this was not day camp
or sleep away camp
or even boot camp
this was death camp
and i do not hear cries
of joy
the blood curdling sounds
were not whistles the counselors wore
they were sounds of
vultures parading in goosesteps
the nazis were very polite
in their violence
their uniforms crisply cut
they bled the fingers that clutched them
the camps so spotless and scrubbed
even the ovens were self-cleaning
i wonder who made them
and the nazis were so well spoken
relocation they preached
the ghetto is so dirty they said
why don't you take a shower
in this stall without drains
they politely requested
scour your soul
clean up your act
they said it so politely
no one resisted
they went willingly
going on away on one-way holiday
their bags packed
with all their perishables
where were the men

where were the women
as children were
merchandised
victimized
they were just following orders
the nazis were just following orders
the jews were just following orders
today's nazis are still following orders
i cannot see myself following orders
i will not follow orders

AT MIDNIGHT

By Radames Ortiz

negroes pound
on burglar bars
with jungle strength
& lizard touch

Adrift in darkness
and jagged light

our machetes
glitter like wet street
shadows

Muscles firm
feet planted
on shagged
carpet

ready to cut,
hack off
Negro limbs

Our own great war
between them & us

throwing rocks, bottles
& broken sticks

pounding heads
like rain
drumming

roof tops

Our own civil battles
black rebellions
mexican triumphs
y aci
the hood became
cemetery of
          blue rage
and white-dove sadness

Por que los calles
are filled with
poor death

as we hang limp
like   small bubbles
of mud & water

our faces drenched
in downstream sewage

Sheep and Goats

By CaLokie

Red eyed derelict
in black
sandals,
pants,
coat,
beard
& skin
stands
to the left of outdoor
Starbuck's table
with palm opened upward
before Peter
in white vestments
talking
on a cellular phone
about tomorrow's ground breaking
ceremony for a new cathedral
while sipping an iced
goat milk latte.

Peter
shakes his head
but does give him directions
to a nearby charity mission.

The mendicant
staggers next
to Simon the Zealot
who hands him
a leaflet explaining
why the gap

between the rich and poor
continues to widen
and their party's revolutionary line
that'll turn things around.

He almost
falls to his knees
stumbling
to another table
but Judas,
standing up,
grabs him
and while holding him up
with one arm
sheepishly stuffs
a $3 roll of dimes
into a jacket pocket
with his free hand
and says, "Now,
what do you want me
to do next, Boss?"

Hands Red. Hands Red.

By Jordan Hurder

I put up my hands to cover my face
they're red.
I put up my hands to cover my eyes
they're red.
from the belly of honesty, guilt rises up
and grips me hard
no tears I can cry
no saltwater tears can sting my face
enough
I'm possessed with the need to erase guilt
with pain, but that's what they did
they erased their guilt
they erased their ignorance with others' pain
they sealed in my rage so much
tighter.
Behind these hands I'm not a fighter.
Why can't I fight against my own?
Who are my own?
The ones I detest so much for being
a part of me, the ones who
will always occupy my blood my skin my corpse
I don't want to fight against myself
I don't want to wage war, so much has
already been waged and I am not ready to die.
I want to apologize, but I'm hiding behind
these hands, I am gripped with a
terrible fear.
My race's past reads like a "shopping list"
of human horror,
yes shopping shopping commercializes atrocities
so just maybe they'll be swept up by the

broom of white capitalism
I'm not a fighter but maybe it's time I realized
just why these hands are red.
I'm not behind them, I'm in them
I am seeing through to their center
And I see blood that could be shed
I see the blood of all humans
and I recognize that I cannot escape this blood
I cannot shed this blood for more will replace it
and no pain will overwhelm
I cannot wage war against this blood because
I will not die without having said that
my blood is red, I can clean it
My blood is red, I will clean it
My hands are red, hands red, hands red.

Apology

By Brandon Backhaus

born German Catholic, southern and white
with evil blood coursing through my veins like napalm
and images of hate
flashing images of forefathers
shadowed behind sky blue eyes
I apologize

Your . . .
holy grounds invaded by knights of a fictitious God
the calls of war on their tongues
a bloodlust on lips
conquering crusaders
blindly executing a political strategy
seeking to spirit away the holiest of land
into the pale and skeletal hands of bishops and cardinals
to steal the sacred sands
STEAL from the hands of God
invasions in the name of Jesus Christ . . .

Your . . .
holy grounds invades by shackle wielding foreigners
with yellow teeth
seeking to cease the beat of your drums
hoarding whole tribes onto ships
body on body in stink and defecation
to a new land where fingers shred
and lashes have nothing to do with eyelids
named in sounds not natural to your beautiful languages
ebony shades blistering under southern skies
enslaved
bleeding in the name of Freedom . . .

Your . . .
holy grounds invaded
as lies slid off rosy tongues
o unfathomable deceit
nearly as many as bullets to buffalo
horrendous agendas of blankets and disease
and trail of dusty tears and cracking heels
to land so barren
dust bowl sodden huts
dignity in the dirt
as crops you taught us how to grow
are harvested on the burial mounds of your ancestors
in the name of Manifest Destiny . . .

Your . . .
holy families dispersed
herded from prosperous city businesses
hauled from crack-of-dawn country ancestral homesteads
to isolation ghettos
ovens manufactured to serve as pillows for
your children
showers pour poison air
bodies of stout bellied men
scrubbed clean with the fat of your women
propaganda read
illuminated in the eradication Aryan nightmare dark
by your skin stretched taught
genocide in the name of a madman . . .

I apologize!
"no races, just classes"
it makes me feel like we are one united in shallow pockets

but then I see the deep roots in the lines of your face like
that of ancient earth spirits
tethered
what am I to say cowering under the ashen face of your
sorrow?
how am I to feel as the rage bubbles to your surface?
what do I know of your ancestral cries?
the stories pacified by the histories of crooks
what do I know but picture books?
no chapter included after the fact
in a vomit-inducing PC gesture
can ever describe the horror
painted in dripping pictures of your blood
caused by the evil in mine
what can I do to atone the sins . . .no! no! more than sins
sin is a word invented to keep us all under the thumb
keep us all in the fields . . .
keep us all on that forsaken trail . . .
keep us all silent and obedient . . .
to keep us all afraid . . .
what can I do to narrow the void?
to construct a crossing to span the bottomless
abyss of hatred created and upheld
to this very day
silent and sinister!
I can't reach you for all the atrocities of
my grandfathers' blue eyes
but I apologize for them
and realize that I must keep my white arm extended
across the canyons of history reaching
and my pale pinkish fist unclenched
and ready to embrace you my brothers.

INTRODUCING MY FRIENDS

Brandon Backhaus:

Brandon Backhaus is originally from New Orleans, Louisiana where he was influenced by a mishmash of cultures from Irish, German, French, Spanish, Cajun, African American, and Vietnamese. He has spent his early adulthood moving from neighborhood to neighborhood around Los Angeles, California. He has settled in the Palms area and is finally feeling a sense of community around him. He is a co-host at Poetic License open-mic poetry reading in Silverlake, California, as well as coordinating and writing reviews for the Poetic License News weekly newsletter. He attends Santa Monica College and is well on his way in his goal of transferring and pursuing a degree in literature. Ultimately he wants to teach English and to someday be privileged enough to pass on his love of word to others. Contact Brandon at bbacchus@prodigy.net

Ray Badders:

If you read these two poems, (Ode to Veronica, Uncle Tom) you'll find my bio between the lines. I am 48 and have been married for 21 years. My wife and I live 5 miles outside of Washington, D.C. with our 5 children. They range in age from 4 - 18. My 18 year old starts at the University of Maryland in August and my 12 year old is away at summer camp this week. My 9 year old is going to Baltimore on Sunday to spend a week with my parents who are in their 80's. My 7 and 4 year old kids are enjoying the kiddie pool that we just blew up with air and filled with water. By the way, all five of my kids are girls!

Steve Baratta:

From NYC Steve is a new force on the Los Angeles Poetry scene. He has featured at many venues in the Southern California area. Steve has moved back to New York City. He is a sensitive poet.

CaLokie:

CaLokie, the nom de plume of Carl Stilwell, is proud to be a Groucho Marxist-John Lennonist from Woody Guthrie's Oklahoma. When I'm not a country teacher, subbing 1-2 days a week for one to two days a week for Los Angeles Unified, I'm a humble country poet the rest of the week. I have poems published in San Fernando Poetry Journal, Struggle,Verve, Pearl, Pemmican, Blue Collar Review. Contact CaLokie at cbstilwell@earthlink.net... thanks for letting me be one of your pips, Cal.

Don Campbell:

Don is a co-host of Barnes and Noble Pasadena, Ca. Tuesday night poetry. He is founder of word process workshops which teaches LA schools. He was a coordinator of the first San Gabriel Poetry festival. He has numerous chapbooks and you can reach him at sensitive @earthlink.net...Thank You, Don.

Michael Grover:

Michael is a dynamic poet and spoken word artist who performs frequently as a feature at numerous LA venues. He has several chapbooks and is in many anthologies. He currently hosts a venue in Philly. Check him out on www.museumofpoetry.com. Thank you, for your piece Michael.

Jerry Hoff:

Am field operations mgr. in Akron area for a security company; will be 65 in November; was raised in Clarksburg, WV; we had segregated schools

Jordan Hurder:

Jordan Hurder, a student at the University of Southern California, is new to the poetry scene, and he has never been published before. He can be seen reading at open mics around the Los Angeles area inadvertently trying to establish himself in hope of lengthening his bio.

Larry Jaffe:

lgjaffe says he was born on a mountaintop in the South Bronx (despite statements to the contrary and that there are no mountains in the Bronx), in the shadow of Yankee Stadium. From the time he could walk he either was going to play baseball, hoops or be a poet or writer. Either that or is the spiritual reincarnation of Davy Crockett. He just could not make up his mind. Jaffe felt he had that mountaintop thing in common with Crockett and his folks once bought him a coonskin cap that he felt ridiculous in, thus took off on this peculiar tangent. He is the product of his own dreams born and bred from Eastern European stock of Russia and Romania.

He has decided that he no longer believe in biographies. And adamantly poses that, "If you want to know who I am read my poetry... why must I trot out lists of places I have appeared and places I have been published or tell you about my childhood dreams to be a beatnik when I grew-up. Ain't that just plain boring? Read the words, read the poetry. It's all in there.The simplicity is I don't want to know what I have done I want to know what I am doing and will do. Another simplicity: the air is letters I breathethem in and simply breathe out poetry."

*With this in mind his biographer, grimacing at the above grammar and language has decided to say that Jaffe has been featured in poetry venues and festivals both throughout the U.S. and abroad. He is very active in the poetry community hosting the very hot ultra chic weekly PoeticLicense series at Zen Restaurant in Silverlake, California. (*www.poetix.net*). Jaffe is also a featured poet for Daimler/Chrysler's Spirit in the Words poetry program. His web sites have won numerous awards (*www.lgjaffe.com*) and feels one of his best creations is the poets4peace site at* www.poets4peace.com. *Each month Jaffe writes a poetry column for www.about.com as the socal poetspondent for their Museletter. He has produced several chapbooks including: Winter Rose, Hates not Natural and Eating the Rain. He has one e-book entitled Jewish Soulfood available from Dead End Street Publications (*www.deadendstreet.com*). His new CD Unprotected Poetry and accompanying book has just been released by PoetWarrior Press (www.poetwarrior .com). Pudding House Publications will be releasing a special book of Jaffe's Greatest Hits along with 12 other poets this June. He is contemplating his career as Davy Crockett poet, once again, having named his computer and truck after Crockett's rifle Ol' Betsy. He says that he is not confused as to which Betsy is which. And poet/critic Mike Cluff once said something very nice about him: : "The best feature I have heard this year anywhere took place at Mc Clain's... Larry Jaffe, gave a wonderful reading that was wow inspiring. His presentation was a* *lively, intense, well-modulated, emotional read: precise and never over-the-top, forced or phony."*

Jimmy Jazz:

Pirate Enclave magazine. Jimmy Jazz is a Poetic Terrorist. He lives in Sand Diego, CA.. He is about to embark on a sports arena poetry tour with Marilyn Manson (filling in the Hole.) He is blessed with dear friends all over the world who sent many responses to the message in a bottle ranging from "What can I do to help?' to 'Get over yourself loser." Thank you for your work Jimmy.
jazz@incommunicado.com

Marion K.:

marion k. (an army brat spending her formative years in Germany and Fort Sam, Texas) now lives and works in rural East Texas with her current husband and four children. Educated at The University of Texas with a Master's in Psychology, she is a Licensed Professional Counselor without patients, except for her two cats, three dogs, squirrels, and an occasional deer.

As she approaches forty, her writing serves as a mechanism for self-connection and MUST write to stay sane, as defined by society. She is published on-line in "The ShallowEND," "Red River Review" where this poem first appeared in February, 2000 and printed in "The Word/artsDFW." She believes in the restorative power of art. "Poetry heals."
Email mdunn@lcc.net to respond to this work.

Stazja McFadyen:

Stazja McFadyen was born in Washington, DC, grew up in Riverdale, Md., moved to Austin, Tx. in 1976. A poet activist, she is best known as publisher/editor of the weekly e-newsletter "Map of Austin Poetry," with 1000 readers in twelve countries. She has served as poetry editor for Austin Downtown Arts magazine; the first Texas correspondent for About.com Museletter; media liaison for Austin Poets at Large; corresponding secretary for Austin Poetry Society for two seasons; board member and venue coordinator for the Austin International Poetry Festival for three years, and founder and host of the monthly East Side Black and White Poets reading series. In addition to three chap books -- "If You Can't Eat 'em, Join 'em" (1997); "Dream Songs" (1998); "Where Would I Be Without You? Love Songs to My Road Atlas (2000) -- her poetry has been published in journals, magazines, anthologies and electronic magazines in the US, Canada, England and Australia. With the recent renaissance of the spoken word art, she has had the good fortune of reading and featuring across the US at festivals, colleges, showcases and live poetry venues. After nearly 25 years, she has returned to Riverdale, Md., and will be participating in a poet/artist collaborative project at the Corcoran Gallery of Art. You are the greatest, girlfriend...Stazja@Aol.com

Katie O'Loughlin:

Katie O'Loughlin travels often and spent a year writing and living in Amsterdam. She has acted for years in plays and musicals and performance pieces in San Diego and Los Angeles. In 1999 and 2000 Katie will be touring performing her spoken word work from her chapbook I Can't Pull it Together Enough to Look Like my Poster. She will be touring throughout California and New York at such venue's as the Atlas Supper Club, Paradise Lounge and the Nuyorican Poets Café. In the fall of 2000 Katie will continue her tour in England, Ireland and Amsterdam. Katie also works with Wordprocess Poets bringing poetry and writing to schools.

RADAMES ORTIZ:

RADAMES ORTIZ is a native Houstonian. He was born and raised in Denver Harbor, a barrio next to Fifth Ward. He is a 21 yr old student and editor of "The Bayou Review," the literary journal for The University of Houston Downtown. His work has appeared in "Metaphor," "diverse city 2000," "Revisions," "Tongue," "LatinoLingo.com," "Elysium" and "The Mesquite Review." He has published a chapbook entitled, "Below the Surface," which was illustrated by artist Tiziano D. Hernandez. Mr. Ortiz is also the recipient of the Fabian Worsham award for poetry

Deon T. Standlee:

Deon T. Standlee grew up in the great state of Texas. Moving around the state just after college, she was finally able to really embrace her heritage as a Southern belle. Moving to Los Angeles in 1993, she never dreamed that she would start reading her poetry and since then has enjoyed features around the LA Basin, Dallas, and Chicago. She is a co-host of PoeticLicense, has helped edit and publish Offering Journal, Fuller Theological Seminary for 6 years and has recently published her own chapbook, "This Ain't Breakfast at Tiffany's...." She currently looks forward to the birth of a new niece and eating lots of Ben and Jerry's with her wonderful boyfriend, Colin.

Xennia

Xennia (Zen-ya) Gittoes-Singh, a.k.a. Running Waters was born in New York, New York. She has lived in New York, New Jersey, Illinois, Colorado, California and currently resides in Virginia. She fell in love with poetry and began to write it when she was nine years old and became an activist at twelve.

She is multi-ethnic (Cherokee, Sikh, French, African-American and Irish) and is an actress, writer, spoken word performance poet and teacher. She has lectured in schools on poetry and racism.

She is published in magazines, newsletters, E-Zines and anthologies. She has published a chapbook entitled Mother Earth's Daughter and produced a CD of the same title with a musical group named Totem providing musical accompaniment. She is currently working on her third volume entitled Homecoming.

She is a wife, (married to William Long) mother, and grandmother.

Xennia is available for readings at personal parties, celebrations, lectures, seminars, workshops and domestic/ international tours, you may contact her at *(804) 776-8184, e-mail Xenpoet2@aol.com*

Xennia

Printed in the United States
31438LVS00001B/12